Beasley

John Tallor

The Penny Detective

Published by G-L-R (Great Little Reads)

Copyright G-L-R

TABLE OF CONTENTS

CHAPTER ONE

I've been feeling guilty recently about how bad I am at my job. Should I be taking money from people for my services? I scored myself around two for professionalism, and one for client satisfaction.

To be fair, I never thought that I was a brilliant detective but on reflection, guessed that maintaining poor to mediocre was OK.

Then, there was the Shoddy factor. My partner, Shoddy, is the brains of the operation and has kept me with my head just above the financial waterline for years. Shoddy has one of the sharpest detective brains I have ever come across; he also cooks most of my meals, so he is like a stepmother to me. Oh yeah, I almost forgot. He is also a raging alcoholic.

My girlfriend, Cynthia, blows hot and cold when it comes to my business activities. There are periods when she enjoys helping me out, but she soon gets bored and because she is loaded with money, she will fly off on a whim to some godforsaken island in the Caribbean with her idle, rich friends. To be fair, she always asks if I want to come, but the day that I say yes will be the day that I hang up my dignity and become a kept man. My dignity took a severe beating a few months ago. I was thinking of flying off to the sun with her, but it was Shoddy who held me back from the brink and brought me to my senses.

What he did was get me so drunk the night before I was due to go that I missed the flight. I don't think Cynthia has forgiven me yet, but what do I care? There are plenty more aristocratic lady millionaires in the world that are just waiting for me to call.

Let's get one thing straight before we start; I am not a music lover and never have been. The thought of going to a rock concert or even a classical concert never entered my head even when I was a teenager. The closest that I ever got to liking a song was listening to German Marching Band Music on BBC Radio Four. I kinda got the message that they were trying to convey, and besides, I have far more in common with soldiers fighting mindless wars and invading places than I ever did with middle-class hippies churning out loud junk music and purposely ripping their Brutus jeans.

Therefore, I was less than overwhelmed when I got a call off Bruce Rush from Red Stripe Entertainment, asking me if I would become the personal bodyguard of a band called Beasley Street for a couple of weeks.

Was I supposed to feel impressed or intimidated? When I asked what they were doing in Liverpool, Rush laughed as if it was obvious.

"The Bees are putting the finishing touches to their comeback album," was the trite reply.

"Bees? Oh yeah, I get it; that's short for Beasley Street, right? Funny, and call me dumb, but I never knew that they had been away," was my confused response.

"It's been twenty years since their last hit, Mr Shannon. Do you want the job or not?"

I asked myself why they even wanted to go through the bother of hiring security, but as always needed the money, so I accepted.

In hindsight, this may have been one of the stupidest decisions of my life, but at least it came at a good hourly rate plus expenses.

The recording studio where I deposited myself the next morning was as plush and high tech as anything you would see in England, or so I was reliably informed by Fire, who was the lead singer of the band and looked like he loved himself. I made the appropriate noises, sat down in the control booth, and listened to the drummer laying down a beat. Everybody seemed to be bouncing their heads in time to the noise, but I never was very good when it came to musical bodily movement. I leered embarrassedly around the room and mouthed "Great," if somebody locked me in eye contact. The drumming seemed to be taking up half the morning. Either that or the plumbing was playing up.

I asked if Fire was his real name, and he asked if I wanted to keep my job, so I shut my mouth and just listened to Connor Crash as he explained my duties. Connor was the bass player and acting manager of the band. He also looked like he was the oldest, and I guessed he was in his late forties. Middle age was not a great time for a rock star, especially one trying to make a comeback and wasn't much of a rock star in the first place.

Connor took me for a vending machine coffee, where he explained my duties and gave me a brief and unwanted history of the band.

"Are you a fan of rock music, Morris?"

I stirred the congealed powdered milk in with my middle finger and pondered the question while the sugar melted.

"No."

He seemed to find this funny and ignored it. "We started Beasley Street in secondary school, I put an advert on the notice board, and it all went from there."

"Fascinating. Why do you need me as security?"

"The thing is, Morris, all of the people that answered the advert lived on my street, which was a big coincidence. We used to practice in a shed at the bottom of the garden using broom handles for microphone stands. We only had one amplifier, and we all played through that. Guitars, bass, and vocals. We were a right old mess."

"Was the name of the street Beasley Street?"

"Yes, how did you guess? We had our first hit after a couple of months and never looked back until the 1970s. Then it all fell apart with the arrival of Punk and New Wave.

"Why do you need security?"

"We went over to Germany after that, like most of the other hard rock bands. We made money, but it wasn't the same. Those Germans don't have any soul. We are back to our best, now, and I think that you are going to see the second coming of the Beasley Boys."

"Why do you need security?"

"Eh? Oh yeah. We need it because the record company insisted on it. It's all a load of old rubbish. Just red tape, so we just got you because you were the cheapest detective in the yellow pages for the area."

"That sums up my life, mate. I think that you will find that not only am I the cheapest, I am also the only detective listed."

"There you go then. That's why you are here. I don't see that you are going to be kept very busy, so just relax and enjoy the vibes. Do you smoke, Man?" He fumbled in his top pocket and brought out a tiny but well packed joint."

"No thanks, Mr Crash. I don't think drugs and security go together. On the other hand, if you have any beer, then I'm all yours."

"Sorry, no beer, man. It slows you down and gives you a fat belly."

"Who are the members of the band, Mr Crash?"

"Please, Morris; we are all friends here. Call me Connor. My friends call me big C."

I wondered what the C stood for but didn't push it as a serious question, even though I had several ideas. "Yeah, my friends call me Moggsy. How many people are in the band?"

"There are four of us. I think you have already met Fire. He's the lead singer, and Buddy Fox is our drummer. I'm the bass player, and on lead guitar, we have the fabulous Greg Angel."

Were these names for real, or had they made them up? Was I interested? Not in the slightest.

Connor started to make his way back to the control room. He walked slowly, as if he had something wrong with either his lower back or his legs. He was wearing unfashionably faded purple loons and a green US military Vietnam combat shirt. It looked authentic but probably wasn't. His hair was long, black, and thin, and featured a bald spot on top that looked like it would probably get bigger on a daily basis. To sum him up, Connor was the sort of person that made you glad that you were not him. For the briefest of moments, he made me contented with my life.

Inside the control room, Fire was on his own playing around with the drum track that we had listened to for half the morning. He was sitting in front of a huge consul and seemed to know what he was doing.

Connor threw himself into a white leather swivel chair next to him and started the head throbbing movement again with his eyes half-closed and his greasy hair swinging. I sat in the corner and wondered if the pubs were open.

"How much of it are you going to use?" Connor's question was aimed at Fire, who seemed not to have heard it. He kept on fiddling with buttons and brought in some other instruments, then took them out again.

"I'm getting squeaks off the bass drum pedal, but nothing that I can't EQ out."

"OK, Fire, you're the boss. When will it be finished?"

"Give me an hour or so, and I will have knocked it into shape."

Connor pushed his chair towards me. He propelled it forward using his legs, which made him look like a spider on a disability pension.

"We will have finished up for the day in maybe a couple of hours. You can go and grab a bite to eat or something, and we will see you later back at the house." He scribbled an address onto a piece of paper. "Here is the house we are staying at. Come over at about nine tonight, and bring your trunks. There is a heated indoor pool. That's going to be your home for the next few days. I bet that this is the easiest money you have ever made."

I simpered and took the paper.

Shoddy lifted his head from the newspaper he was reading when I got back home. The good thing about my partner was that not only did he have a brilliant mind for solving cases, but he lived in the next flat to mine and wasn't such a bad cook.

"Why didn't you tell me that you had got a new job?"

I sat down at the table and poured myself a cup of tea. "Because last night, when I came home, you were too drunk, and this morning when I left, you were sleeping it off."

"That's still no excuse. By the look on your face, it didn't go that well. What's the problem?"

"No problem, Shod. Is there anything to eat?"

He got up, went over to the stove, and spooned in what looked like stew from a pan into two ceramic bowls. He brought them over, sat down at the table, and sparked up a cigarette. As I ate, I filled him in on my morning.

He continued to mumble about not being asked before I signed a contract, but he almost choked on a piece of lamb when I mention the name of the band."

"Beasley Street? That bunch of losers? I suppose that you know the story about why they faded into obscurity?"

"Yeah, they said that it was due to people liking other forms of music. They went to Germany and played there."

"More like the fact that the lead singer was accused of murder and their record company couldn't handle the negative publicity and chucked them off the label."

"They never told me that."

"Well, let's face it, Moggsy. They either thought that you already knew, or if you didn't, they weren't going to bring it up."

"How did you know about it?"

"Because I was part of the police team that investigated it."

Shoddy had once been a high-ranking cop. He was at the height of his professional career when I first met him, but it had been downhill from then on. A mixture of alcohol and heroin had fuelled his downfall, and his attempted suicide culminated in him being pensioned off. It was a case of their loss and my gain, though it was a fine line that we walked between being sober and brilliant or blind drunk and useless.

I waited as he lit another cigarette, wiped up his gravy with some crusty bread, then settled back in his chair. He wiped his mouth with the back of his hand and looked at the ceiling as he tried to summon up the past.

"I was just a kid at the time, not long on the force, and still wet behind the ears. Believe it or not, I was a bit of a fan of Beasley Street, and I had bought their first hit album. Still got it as it happens. It's in that box over there." He pointed to an old naval chest underneath the window that I had never seen him open in all of the years I had known him.

"Part of the attraction was that they were from Liverpool. Back in them days, all you needed to do was tune up a guitar, and some London record company would give you a record deal. I guess it was the Beatle effect. Everybody was looking for the new John, Paul, George, and Ringo. Beasley Street?" His brow became furrowed. "Well, they were the Fire, Connor, Buddy, and?"

"Greg:"

"Yeah, they were the Fire, Connor, Buddy, and Greg of the music industry. The names hardly rolled off your tongue, and they were not like the Beatles or any of the other Liverpool bands. Even their hair was longer than the other bands."

"How do you mean?"

"It was all about pop music in them days. All of the lyrics were girl meets boy sort of thing. Not Beasley Street. They were very political. Ban the bomb and down with the rich. That sort of thing. Of course, the rich kids loved them, and that was when it happened."

"What happened?"

"We got an anonymous call in the early hours of the morning about people leaving a house in Litherland and making a noise. We thought that it was a disgruntled neighbour, and I was sent with my sergeant to investigate the disturbance. When we arrived at the house, the party must have broken up. It's usually the case that neighbours start to complain as people are making a noise when they are leaving. We were about to drive back to the station when I noticed that the door was open. We went inside. There was the body of a naked man in the swimming pool at the back of the house. The lead singer of the band, Fire, was unconscious at the side of the pool. We called for backup, and all hell broke loose."

I fished the piece of paper out of my pocket. "Did you say Litherland? What was the address?"

"I can't remember the exact number, but it was one of those posh houses down Lightfoot Street."

"Number twelve."

"Yeah, possibly, but how do you know it?"

"Because that's the address where I am going in a bit. The band is staying there. They told me that it had a swimming pool but missed out that it had a history of dead bodies floating in it."

"Just the one, mate."

"That's one too many for me, Shod. Who owns the house?"

"I have no idea. But what I do know is the body in the pool finished the band. Fire was arrested but got off due to insufficient evidence. That didn't stop the press from having a field day. They crucified the band for weeks, and in the end, they slinked off and disappeared."

"Germany."

"What?"

"Apparently, they went to Germany and played over there."

"That must have been worse than going to prison." Shoddy poured us both another cup of tea.

"Who was the body, Shod?"

"Now that's the funny thing. Nobody recognised him."

"How is that possible?"

"According to the band, lots of fans gate-crashed their parties and the security was nonexistent. Nobody associated with Beasley Street could give us a name, and nobody from the general public came forward about a missing person.

The case just got filed away in police records. It was the newspapers that wouldn't let it go. They hounded the band and hounded their record label. I felt sorry for them in a way. I was present when CID interviewed Fire; obviously, that's not his real name, but I got the impression that he didn't have it in him to kill anybody. Besides, he had so much alcohol inside him that he physically couldn't have done it."

"Was anybody else suspected?"

"This is Croxley, not Scotland Yard. When we realised we didn't have much of a case, we gave up. Just one more murder. Besides, in those days, we had a gangland war going on, and bodies were turning up in shop doorways on a weekly rota."

"Yeah, I guess those types of parties had a load of illegal drugs floating around. Who knows what went on? You never told me how he was killed."

"Oh, that? It was a hard blow to the back of his head. It could have been an accident I suppose. No murder weapon was found. There was a rather large statue of Eros that could have been used as a weapon, but there were no fingerprints or traces of skin on it from the body."

"Wiped?"

"Maybe."

"What was your opinion?"

"Me? I didn't think that he did it, but somebody did, and we will probably never find out who. I have always had a nose for murder and this incident smelt bad. It could have been an accident, but he was naked and his clothes were never found. It was weird, but that's the music business. Do you fancy a swift drink before you go to work?"

"Go on then, but just the one."

CHAPTER TWO

I took the not very scenic coastal road to Litherland. Driving up the A565 was never a pleasant experience. Why? Because no matter what season it was, the area was still grim with little or no charm. These days you couldn't even see the coast. It was just a series of housing estates that neither had the charm of the old working-class terraced houses of the 1950s or the class of the mature detached houses of the rich people that lived in Litherland, which was my destination.

As a boy, I knew from my experiences that the sea was always too rough and dirty to swim in, but the course, grassy embankment that lined the shore was a great place to come at night, set up a tent, light a fire, and go fishing. We never caught anything, but it made childhood as near idyllic as you could get, living in Croxley.

I wasn't the least bit phased by what Shoddy had told me about the band's history and the body in the pool. Even as I turned into the long drive of number twelve Lightfoot Street, I was still convinced that all I had to do was spend a bit of time with the band, pick up a fat wedge of money and go home. As always, I had completely miscalculated the situation.

The house was geometrically aligned to the smallish garden that was well kept but lacking in anything natural like a bush or a flower. The house was a cube of gleaming white stone that looked like a highly polished municipal office building. The windows were conspicuously lacking in any curtains or blinds, but there was only one lit up. It burned brightly at the side of the heavy oak front door, which was open. The figure of a woman stood silhouetted against the harsh lighting inside. She turned her head to look out of the window as I opened the door of my car, then disappeared.

I got out and walked across the noisy white gravel. As I got closer, the silhouette took on the form of a lanky blonde woman, dressed in a loosely flowing kaftan. She had moved to the door and didn't look happy. Neither did the woman who joined her. This one was a redhead; small and thin, wearing jeans and a t-shirt.

"You must be the detective hired to protect us," said the redhead. Did I detect a trace of sarcasm in her voice? I gave them both my best detective leer.

"You two ladies don't look in high spirits. What's the trouble?"

They turned and walked into the house, and I followed them. We went down a rather scruffy hallway and entered a big, but untidy room that looked like it served as a lounge. The drum kit and piano set up in the corner could have meant that it also served as a practice room. From what I had heard from the band earlier on, they certainly needed it.

The blonde went over to the window and stood looking out. The redhead sat down on one of the three settees that littered the space next to the fireplace. I could think of nothing better to do than sit down as well.

"I'm Hilary Crash, Mr Shannon. I'm Greg's wife, and this is Mercy Austin, who is Fire's wife. I'm afraid you are going to need your detective skills tonight." I noticed that her lips were trembling.

"What's happened?"

"The boys have gone missing."

"Which boys?"

"Our boys. Fire and Greg went out for a drive and haven't come back."

"When was that? I was speaking with them less than three hours ago."

"Then it must have been just after you left." The blonde had moved from the window and stood over me. She had accusation in her eyes. "Excuse me for being ignorant in these matters, but aren't you getting paid to protect my husband?"

"Your husband and the rest of the band."

She snorted at this. "I think that you will find that in this band, the only one that is worth any money in Fire. He is the only one that has had even a sniff of a solo career. He only agreed to make this comeback tour to help Greg and the others."

Hilary Crash avoided eye contact. "Yes, it's brutal, but it's true. Without Fire, there would never have been a comeback album. Did you know that Fire has recently had a hugely successful album in the USA and Japan?"

I had to confess that I didn't, but I also didn't want to seem like a musical idiot, so I changed the subject. "It's only been a couple of hours. Maybe they have gone to the pub. People do that, you know."

Mercy Austin lit up what looked suspiciously like a joint and blew smoke in my face. I hate smoking, but in my job, it's an occupational hazard. I just know that sometimes in the future, it will not be a bullet or a knife that gets me but some disease from passive smoking. She sat down as if the first couple of puffs had turned her legs to jelly.

"They have not gone to any pub, Mr Shannon. They have been kidnapped. God, how I wish we had never agreed to this. It's alright for the rest of them; they are poor as church mice, so who would want to get money out of them. I wish we were poor again." She looked around the large room. It was untidy, but even I could see it had been expensively decorated and furnished. "Having lots of money is a curse, don't you think, Mr Shannon?"

"Not really, Mercy. Poor people have got their problems too. I spend a lot of time with them. I should know."

She looked at me full in the face. Her blue eyes were slightly misted with tears, but she seemed to be seeing me for the first time since I arrived. She fished into her handbag, brought out a piece of paper with writing on it, and threw it onto the coffee table.

"What's that?"

"Read it yourself; it's what rich people have to go through to pay for our sins."

I picked it up. It had been written in block capitals using a red crayon.

TO MERCY AUSTIN

WE HAVE FORD AUSTIN AND CONNOR CRASH, AND FOR THE NEXT TWENTY FOUR HOURS THEY ARE SAFE IF YOU FOLLOW THESE INSTRUCTIONS

DO NOT INVOLVE THE POLICE

WE WANT ONE HUNDRED THOUSAND POUNDS IN USED BANK NOTES TO BE DELIVERED IN A BAG ONTO THE BACKSEAT OF A CAR PARKED ON ERMINE ROAD. IN CROXTETH.

YOU CAN IDENTIFY THE CAR BECAUSE IT WILL HAVE A LARGE X PAINTED IN WHITE ON THE BACK SEAT. IT WILL BE CLOSE TO THE TELEPHONE BOX ON THE CORNER. DON'T WASTE YOUR TIME CHECKING LICENCE PLATES BECAUSE IT WILL HAVE BEEN STOLEN.

THE MONEY SHOULD BE DELIVERED BY YOU ON WEDNESDAY AT NINE AM.

AFTER YOU HAVE PUT THE MONEY INTO THE CAR KEEP WALKING

DO NOT LOOK BACK

DO NOT HAVE ANYBODY WATCHING THE STREET

IF YOU DO NOT FULFIL ANY OF OUR REQUESTS.

ON THURSDAY, YOU AND HILARY CRASH WILL BE RECEIVING PIECES OF YOUR HUSBANDS IN A BOX. WE WILL START WITH FINGERS.

FOLLOW THE INSTRUCTIONS TO THE LETTER, AND YOU WILL RECEIVE YOUR, HUSBANDS, BACK THE SAME DAY

"Ford Austin?"

"That's Fire, my husband," said Mercy. "His parents had a weird sense of humour. Why do you think his stage name was Fire?"

"How many people knew what his real name was?"

"How should I know? Not many."

The cogs in my brain were already whirling. Could it be somebody close to the band that had written the ransom note? The next question was obvious. "Have you got the money?"

"Yes, of course. It's in the house. Fire doesn't believe in banks, so we keep most of our money in the safe. We keep it in cash and gold and old paintings. That was one of his hobbies."

"What?"

"Collecting valuable paintings. We have a couple of paintings by Constable."

"Are you planning to pay?"

"Of course, what else is there to do?"

I had to admit that on the surface, it seemed that to pay was the only solution. The timescale was too short for the police to set up anything serious in an attempt to catch the kidnappers. I wondered what I could do.

Hilary Crash made her excuses and said that she had a headache and was going for a lie-down. That left Mercy and me.

"We have until nine tomorrow to come up with a plan."

"Do you really think that what we need is a plan, Mr Shannon?"

"Why, what do you suggest?"

"I suggest that we pay up and get on with our lives."

"I'm assuming that you are only paying half of the ransom. Does Hilary Crash have that much spare money?"

"No."

"What does that mean?"

"It means that I pay, and we settle up in some way later. I hardly think that Hilary would be too bothered if she got any of Connor's fingers through the post. They don't have that much of a marriage."

"I see."

"I don't think that you do, but there again you don't need to. Hilary was one of the fans that used to hang around. She was pretty enough to be spotted by Connor and clever enough to get him to marry her. Connor was the star, but Hilary ruled their relationship. Still does, but I think she feels like she has wasted her life, especially after the German fiasco. None of them had that much talent. Fire was the voice of the band and could have become famous with just a load of session musicians in the background. Oh, and did I tell you that he wrote all of their hit songs?"

"Why did he come back and join them again?"

"Oh, the so-called comeback of Beasley Street? I was always against it, but my husband is easily led and was nostalgic for the old days. Call it unfinished business if you like."

I didn't like to say but I wondered if it was a bit of guilt after being investigated by the police for murder. There was an awkward silence while I mulled over whether to bring it up. Luckily, Mercy had her mind on other things.

"From the look on your face, Mr Shannon, I can see that you are thinking of doing something."

I didn't bother telling her what I was really thinking; I kept silent and waited for her to tell me what she wanted to do. At least that way, I couldn't be blamed for whatever happened to her husband and his mate. A bit insensitive, I know, but what the hell, I had only just met them, and they certainly weren't friends.

"What's your plan, Mr Shannon? Do you think that we can follow the kidnappers?"

"Anything is possible. I know Ermine Road. I think I know where the telephone box is. If I'm not wrong, there is a car park across the road on another street called Wayland Close. It's one of those multi-storey things."

"Don't you think that somebody will be watching the car?"

"I would put money on it." I looked at my watch. It was coming up to midnight. Time to start earning my money. "Of course, if I went early enough and found a good spot, then there is a good chance that nobody will see me."

"How early? Your bedroom is ready here; do you want to be there an hour before I have to go? Or are you going to come with me and then hide?"

These people had no idea about how criminal minds worked. But there again, why should they? I got up out of the chair. "I was thinking more about going now. They would not think that anybody would be stupid enough to hide all night."

"I'm sure you are right about that, Mr Shannon. It does sound a bit over the top."

As I left the house, I wondered what the bed would have been like. It would certainly have been better than the car park I was going to.

I telephoned Shoddy as I was on my way. He took in the information in silence and didn't offer any advice other than to come home, not get involved in any kidnapping, and just take the money. To be fair, I was still considering it after driving into the car park. It was early morning and not a soul about. I found myself a spot and looked over at Ermine Road from between the rusty iron railings on the first level.

The street had just a smattering of cars, but there was a big space in front of the telephone booth. My hiding place was not very good, and I thought long and hard about how I could best camouflage myself. In the end, I gave up, sat in my Riley Elf, and read an old newspaper for a bit.

At about two in the morning, I went down to the telephone box and looked up. I could just about see my car on the other said of the railings, but at the angle that I was, it was impossible to see the newspaper that I had hung over the steering wheel. It was a makeshift plan, but unfortunately, it was all that I had. I hoped that being in the car park so early would be the key to being able to follow whoever was going to pick up the money.

By two-thirty, I was fast asleep, and by six o'clock, I was shaking uncontrollably with the cold. I hated my job and contented myself by listing in my head the top ten reasons why.

CHAPTER THREE

The money pick-up happened so quickly and smoothly that it was difficult not to admire the planning. I was, of course, wide-awake at eight o'clock and staring dry-mouthed through the steering wheel and out of my windscreen at the street below. Whoever had picked Lightfoot Street had wanted somewhere that was not too crowded with commuters and had good access for a speedy getaway.

I noticed the chocolate brown Nissan 120Y go past the phone box and didn't pay much attention. After it had gone around the block twice, I felt the adrenalin rising, and when it parked exactly in front of the telephone box, I checked my watch. It was ten to nine. Perfect timing.

I couldn't tell whether it was a man or a woman who got out, but my instincts told me the build was either a man or a gorilla. The person that walked towards the multi-storey car park was dressed in a dark blue anorak with the hood pulled up. A pair of tinted glasses masked the eyes, and a tartan scarf covered the mouth.

The person disappeared from view, and I assumed had entered the car park via the automatic barrier. I wondered if they would check the first level. Nobody appeared, and I waited to see if Mercy Austin would be on time.

She appeared at two minutes to nine and had a black bag in her hand. As she passed by the Nissan, she glanced at the back seat, quickly opened the door, threw the bag inside and walked away.

As soon as she had gone around the corner, the person in the anorak ran across the street and started the car up. I sprang into action, reversed my Riley Elf out of the parking space, and drove speedily down the ramp to the barrier. It was here that I realised that I hadn't been as smart as I should have been.

I couldn't find the ticket to put in the machine to lift the barrier. When I eventually did find it, I realised that somebody had put putty in the slot where the card should have gone. In short, somebody had sabotaged the ticket machine.

There was not much that I could do. I had two straight choices, either press the alarm and wait half of the morning for somebody to let me out, or do it the spectacular way. Part of me wanted to wait, but I realised that I had been in the car park overnight and didn't have the eight pounds to pay.

I eyed up the barrier. It didn't look that solid. I reversed a bit up the ramp and headed straight for it. This was something that I had always wanted to do, and as the wood splattered and pieces flew by, I had a wide smile on my face fuelled by the feel-good factor. I felt like James Bond for a few seconds, but then reality kicked in. I realised that I had very little chance of finding the Nissan or the money.

It was ten past nine by my watch. Ten minutes since the kidnapper had ridden off. I wondered if he had seen me and fixed the barrier because of it but thought it through and came to the conclusion that he had just done this for extra security. If I thought that the car park was a good place to observe the drop-off, then why not the kidnapper. He must have planned it before. Either that, or he always carried around with him a tub of quick setting putty.

The area that I was in was called Croxteth and had a pretty bad reputation for crime. I knew it reasonably well, and I knew that the road that the Nissan had taken was straight and didn't have that many streets running off it. It was an area of boarded-up houses, closed businesses, and the occasional fried chicken joint and Chinese takeaway. This was drug city a-go-go, and then some. I had spent many an hour in these streets watching houses as unfaithful wives and husbands went about the business of cheating on their spouses. My aim was to get some pictures of the dirty deeds. I would say that my success rate was less than satisfactory, but the money I received was adequate to keep me from getting a proper job. I got rid of the memories and concentrated on where I was heading. The streets were waking up, and unwashed youths in shell suits, Velcro, and denim were walking around with bleary dead eyes trying to piece together what they would do for the rest of the day. The pavements were strewn with polythene cups and empty burger containers broken up by the more sophisticated pizza boxes and easily identifiable silver Chinese takeaway cartons.

I loved Liverpool. Nowhere else in the world had the downtrodden atmosphere of these streets. There was something blissfully poetic about it. These people were not villains or losers. They were the bad blood that throbbed through the veins of the city. They were the scallies that would steal your money and give you a good kicking, but also give you their last chip if you were hungry.

I was fast approaching the motorway, and if I went on it, I knew that I had lost the money and would have to go and tell Mercy Austin the bad news. I went all the way around the roundabout, avoiding the motorway turning, and headed back the way I came. It was a long shot, but as there were only half a dozen or so streets going off the one I was on, then maybe it was worth taking a look. I also knew that most of them were dead ends and didn't lead anywhere.

I needed a bit of luck, and as I went down the first street called Wellman Close, I thought that I had just received it. There was a Datsun 120Y parked between a rubbish skip and a cement mixer. It was the right make and the right colour but had no wheels and was jacked up on bricks. Even in my wildest dreams, I couldn't imagine why the kidnappers would do something like this. Maybe they were compulsive about their oil and air filters being clean or had become attached to the wheels and took them home as a memento of the heist.

I did a U-turn and got back on Wayland. My luck was definitely not in on the rest of the streets, and I was about to give up when I noticed a piece of wasteland with a grass track leading to it. I had nothing better to do, so I parked the Elf and made my way along it on foot.

I passed a disused burger van and a fenced-off scrap yard with a sign claiming that good money would be paid for 'Old Bangers,' as long as the seller had the logbook proving ownership.

Beyond the scrap yard with its red rusting gates and howling German Shepherds, there was a muddy swamp with the shells of a row of derelict terraced houses that separated it from the motorway, which flowed noisily past.

This was the sort of desolate place that would come alive with all kinds of low life scum who only came out at night. Now, the only other human that I could see was a woman in a black leather coat, white stilettos, and very little else. She wore her hair in a beehive and resembled a UN refugee from a wacky grab a granny disco. She was slowly navigating the large holes in the ground with a loaded supermarket shopping trolley in front of her that was full of rattling gin bottles. It wasn't a hollow rattle, so I assumed that they were full and hot. There was a story in there somewhere, but I didn't have time to find it.

She managed to reach the row of decrepit houses and disappeared through a gap in the wall. On the right of the gap was a chocolate brown Datsun 120Y. As I got closer, I realised that it was a Datsun Sunny. I also realised that there was something wrong with the driver who wasn't moving much.

He was leaning back in the driver's seat with his mouth open and his teeth locked into a snarl. His top denture plate had dropped and was slightly jutting out from his mouth, giving him a kind of Bugs Bunny vibe, which was cute yet macabre at the same time. There was a large letter X scrawled in white paint on the backseat but not the bag that Mercy Austin had thrown in.

The driver was a big man. He had short ginger hair, blue eyes, and a shocked look on his face. I imagined that the reason for this was the knife sticking out of his neck. There was a dark blue anorak on the passenger seat, and I went through the pockets looking for clues as to his identity.

My detective skills kicked in, and I tried to figure out why he had taken the anorak off. He was wearing it when he drove out of Lightfoot Street. I concluded that he could have stopped here to wait for an accomplice? If so, had he been double-crossed? This didn't look good for the kidnapped boys from Beasley Street.

The keys of the vehicle still dangled from the ignition, but there was no address attached to them, just an empty brown leather pouch. I went around to the front of the car and made a note of the registration number. I assumed that it had been stolen, but Shoddy could check through one of his cop mates.

I searched inside the pockets of the anorak. They revealed a bar of dark Cadbury's chocolate, some nail clippers, and a half-broken penknife that wouldn't close properly. I went through his trouser pockets and found nothing in his side pockets, but in his back pocket, there was a brown leather wallet with a chewed up business card inside.

The card read

Property Growth Assurance

For all of your Financial Needs

Tel 051 659 222

Or why not pop in for a chat. We are at 9 Hawthorn Street Manchester

I put the wallet and the business card in my pocket and made my way back to the Elf.

I stopped at a telephone box on Wayland and made three calls. One was to Mercy Austin to say that I was following up a lead and not to worry. She chose to ignore my advice and hammered me with loads of questions. I didn't answer any of them but told her I would stop by her house later.

The second call was to the police. I passed one of their squad cars travelling at high speed with its lights and siren blazing as I made my way to Manchester and the offices of Property Growth. I hoped that when I came back to Croxley, it would be with something other than full life cover and health insurance.

I had run out of change by the third call and had to reverse the charges. Shoddy wasn't too pleased, but I gave him the registration number of the Datsun Sunny and made him promise to find out the owner as soon as he could.

CHAPTER FOUR

Property Growth was on the third floor of an impressive office block off Piccadilly Gardens in the city's northern quarter. Parking was tight near the centre, and I eventually was forced to slip into a spot in front of a parking metre. I wondered if I should risk it but decided that fifty pence for half an hour was worth it, if only for the fact I could claim a pound back on expenses. That's the sort of guy I am, cheap and cheerful. There was a left-hand drive mustard coloured Mercedes parked on the pavement in front of the office. The driver was obviously trying to make a statement. I looked at my Riley Elf and wondered what sort of a statement I was making.

I took the lift up to the third floor and was interrogated by a middle-aged lady with dyed blonde hair and a heavily faked suntan. She assured me that Mr Gittins was extremely busy and only did appointments by appointment, which I guess was logical. However, I insisted, and my argument that it was a matter of life and death eventually led her to make a call to see if he was free.

I did not doubt that he would be, and within ten seconds of the call, he appeared like an apparition from a door at the side. He was in his late thirties, with an overly non-robust physique and an expensive suit. I was immediately impressed by how shiny his patent leather shoes were and how exaggeratedly firm his handshake was.

He had just the slightest smell of alcohol and cigarette smoke and a larger than life smile. He lifted a flap, ushered me behind the reception counter and told his receptionist to hold all calls. For some reason, she seemed to find this funny. I followed him into his private office, which was dominated by a large oak desk and two even larger leather swivel chairs.

He sat down and swivelled, and I joined him. It eased any of the tensions out of our meeting. "What is the nature of your business, Mr?"

"I'm a private detective. My name is Morris Shannon."

"Stop right there. You know, of course, that for people in your profession, there is a high risk that you will die and leave your wife or live-in partner in a very precarious position. Do you have insurance cover? If not, don't you think that you owe it to her?"

"I'm not married."

He sat back, put his hands together in a sort of praying motion, and examined the ceiling. As if he had been struck by a revelation, he locked eye contact again. He was having a eureka moment. "You have no dependents?"

"No."

"Then, you are obviously in need of a wealth-creating scheme that will give you a nice little nest egg for early retirement. Did you know that you don't need a lump sum to invest in a low to medium risk unit trust scheme? We can take it out of your bank every month."

"I'm not here about my finances."

"Most people who I speak to are not initially interested in putting money aside for when they pass or saving for the future. Are you saying that you are rich and don't expect to die?"

"No, I'm not saying that."

"Are you telling me that you don't want to retire early?"

"Yeah, that would be nice, but..."

"Do you think that the state pension will be enough to live on?"

I laughed at this. "No, I'm not saying that, but I am here to investigate kidnapping and murder." I placed the business card on the desk. "This card was found at the scene of the murder, and I would like to ask you if you can tell me who it belonged to."

"Mmm, that does seem to be serious, Morris. I have a few agents working for me. I'm sorry, but I can't tell you who the owner of this particular business card is. We give them to our agents in batches of a hundred. Can you describe him?"

"Yes, he was around six foot three. Slightly smaller than me, with red hair. Fairly well built."

"That would be our Mr Blake. David Blake. Did you say that he had been kidnapped?"

"No, Mr Gittins, he has been murdered."

"Ah, I see. Now when I said our Mr Blake, I wasn't being accurate. I had to let him go last year. He left by mutual agreement. Most do, you know. They think that selling life assurance is going to be easy. They see me driving around in a fantastic car and think that anybody can do it, but they are wrong. It takes talent. It takes talent and drive. It takes long hours walking the streets and pounding doors. It takes…"

"Yeah, OK, I get the picture. You are saying that David Blake didn't have what it takes, and you had to let him go."

"Didn't have what it takes and also a bit of a con artist."

"In what way?"

"He had been taking cash deposits on new policies and not passing them through the books. I found out by chance when somebody came into the office to cancel a policy and wanted her money back. When I told her that we don't take money at the door, she threatened to go to the police. Most unfortunate. It took charm and a great deal of talking to stop her. I sacked David on the same day. I only took him on as a favour to a mutual friend."

"Are you saying that you knew him well?"

That wiped the smile off his face, and he began to look uneasy and not in control for the first time.

"Look, Morris, are you trying to say that I am involved in any way with this? What did Mr Blake do?"

"He took a substantial sum of money off my client and kidnapped two people."

He whistled dramatically at that. "Wow, I would never have thought that David would have had the guts for something like that. It just goes to show how wrong you can be."

"From what happened to Blake, I am fairly sure that he wasn't alone. His partner has more than likely double-crossed him."

"That partner would not be me, Morris."

"This mutual friend. Do you have a name and address?"

"She is not a friend. More of a client, but you know from your own business that sometimes lines can get crossed and clients can become friends."

"Not really, Mr Gittins. What is the name and address?"

"Her name is Breanna Holcomb. She's an actress and was also a singer in a local beat band. I met her when she was doing the rounds of the clubs and sold her a pension. Of course, she only paid the first couple of months and let it lapse, but we kind of clicked."

I wondered if his wife knew. "Have you got an address?"

"It's in Hale. I haven't seen her since I was forced to let David go, so I don't even know if she still lives there. You know what these young girls are like."

"Why, how old is she?"

"In her twenties. She looks older than her age. Are you trying to imply something, Morris?" He laughed to take the tension out of his obvious discomfort, but I didn't give him the benefit of a reply.

"And the address?"

"Do you think that she is involved in this?"

"I need the address to find out. I'll send you a postcard with my opinion if you want."

He sneered at this. "I went a couple of times to her place, and as I said, she is a drifter that one, and I would expect her to be long gone."

He scribbled something down on a piece of paper and handed it to me.

I thanked him and headed for the door. Before I could open it, he had run past me and almost knocked me out of the way. He smiled apologetically. "Before you go, Morris; I know that you are not interested in life assurance and savings, but just for the record."

"For the record?"

"Yes, just for the record, can you tell me why not?"

"Why not what?"

"Why a man like you in your profession doesn't think that he needs savings or at least burial money."

I laughed at this one. "I told you. I don't have any dependents, so as far as I am concerned, they can throw me into a trashcan when I die. I don't need to save money because I have a dad who is a multimillionaire who will eventually die and leave me all of his money. Satisfied?"

He looked deflated but opened the door.

"Do you have the address of your dad? Maybe I can have something to interest him."

I never bothered replying. I guess business was bad, or he just had a naturally desperate disposition.

Before getting into my car, I found a pub and had a beer and a beef and mustard sandwich. The bread was slightly stale, and the beer flat and warm. It reminded me of my life. Potentially great from a distance, but on closer examination not up to the required standard. I phoned Shoddy up with the change I had received off the friendly barmaid who made up for the poor late lunch.

He had been busy; the car had been reported as stolen and belonged to somebody called Caleb Ward. I wasn't too shocked or disappointed by this bit of news.

I filled Shoddy in on what I had been doing and set off in the car for Hale and, hopefully, a surprise appointment with Breanna Holcomb.

CHAPTER FIVE

The little, black and white, wooden bungalow was in the grounds of a much larger house, which was at the end of a trim and well-kept street of detached monoliths on the outskirts of Hale.

There were no lights on in the bungalow, and I wasn't too surprised when my knocking didn't bring a result. The main house or semi-mansion was a different prospect, and as I walked towards it, I could hear music drifting out from one of the ground floor windows, all of which were slightly open. I didn't recognise the music, but it sounded like some type of opera. I think the people singing were Italian.

I rang the front doorbell, and as if it were attached in some way to the stereo system, the music stopped abruptly. I could hear extremely slow footsteps coming towards me and instinctively knew that I was being scanned through the spy hole.

I must have passed my physical exam because the door opened slightly before the guard chain kicked in. An old man wearing dark glasses looked through the gap. He had a judgmental mouth and a Groucho Marx moustache.

"Make this quick."

"Make what quick?"

"Whatever your spiel is."

"I don't have any spiel."

"You know what I mean. Is it windows or insurance that you are trying to sell me?"

Insurance again? I wondered if Harry Gittins had tried his sales technique on this guy when he visited Breanna Holcomb. "I am not trying to sell anything. I am a private detective and I am trying to trace a young lady called Breanna Holcomb. Is she in?"

He closed the crack in the door slightly as if the name had disturbed him. His expression hardened, and I got a distinct impression that he would have preferred me to be selling something.

"Are you one of her dropout friends?"

"No. My name is Morris Shannon. I'm a private detective. Is she in? Could I have a word?"

"What has she done?"

"I am investigating a very serious incident, and maybe Breanna can help me with my enquiries."

I heard a click as the chain was taken out. "I knew it. I warned her that she was going to end up in prison. Is it robbery or murder?"

He swung the door open, and I got the full effect of his presence. He was slightly silhouetted against the darkness I was now standing in and the bright lights of the hall. He wore a red and silver smoking jacket and extremely tight and revealing beige riding jodhpurs. His hair was black and greased back, and the monocle stuck in his left eye gave him a vibe that dated back to the roaring twenties, or at least to an era before I was born. I pushed my luck.

"Can I come in? It is a private matter."

He stepped to one side and pushed the door open wider. "Help yourself, but make it quick I have more important things to do with my evenings than talk about Miss Holcomb."

The house was massive and under furnished to the point beyond minimalism. Everything was modern except the owner, who was a veritable retro icon to the age of the speakeasy and illegal hooch. We crossed a wide hall and entered what I assumed was the living room. It smelt of spice and fried chicken. Above the ornate designer fireplace sat an almost full-size painting of my host, though in his younger days. Above his head in red was the word Gonzo. He cut a dashing figure. He saw me looking. "That was back in the days when I only had to look at a chick, and she was putty in my hands. They called me Gonzo because I was fast at chatting up women" He picked up on my confusion. "Short for Gonzales. Do you know the song Speedy Gonzales?"

"Yeah, vaguely."

"Do you like fine art, Mr Shannon?"

"No."

"Well, that's killed the niceties. Do sit down, and tell me what this is all about."

We sat in designer settees that were facing each other with a coffee table in the middle. There was a decanter of something that looked rather interesting on a silver tray on the table. The two glasses demanded to be filled, but he chose to ignore them.

"Where do you want to begin, Mr Shannon?"

"We could start with your name."

"Ah, yes. My name is Albert Cross. Cross by name but not by nature." He smiled and waited for my compliant laughter at his attempted joke.

I could never laugh to order, so I just nodded my head and showed my teeth. It was sufficient to satisfy him.

He leaned forward, conspiratorially, and whispered. "What has she done this time?"

"This time? What sort of things has she been doing that you know of? The only thing that I know is that she may or may not be involved in a kidnapping."

"Kidnapping, eh? Who is the kid?"

"I mean kidnapping in its general form. We are talking about two men that have gone missing. I think that Breanna could be involved, but I can't be one hundred percent certain. Are you telling me that she doesn't live here anymore?"

"Yes, I rather think that I am, Mr Shannon. She got too much for me to handle and what with the other business that happened, I had to give her notice to quit the bungalow."

"Are you at liberty to tell me what she did?"

"Apart from ruining my life while she was here? Yes, I am at liberty to tell you, but if you want some sort of character detail, I can tell you that Breanna Holcomb had the demeanour of a spoilt brat. She claimed that she came from a poor working-class family, and at first, I believed her. But then…"

"But then?"

"I took her in because she paid three months up front, and her reference was pretty good. I have to admit that the money came in very handy. The upkeep of this place is not easy, and a lot of people had seen the bungalow and weren't interested." He hesitated as if he was considering whether he could trust me. "Its damp inside, and there are the early signs of woodworm. She didn't seem to mind and didn't argue about the price. When she offered three months in advance, I snapped her hand off."

"You say that you had a reference?"

"I let the house through an agency. They insist on references otherwise, even if I wanted to, I couldn't rent through them. It's safer like that, so I don't mind. For Breanna, it wasn't a reference; it was a letter from a guarantor. She had no job. She was an actress and was in between roles. She had been on the BBC, you know. I was impressed by that."

"You say that she was not ideal as a tenant. Why was that?"

"I'm no party-pooper, Mr Shannon. We have had some rather noisy cocktail parties at the lodge from time to time, and I throw a very nice whist and bridge evening, but nothing like her."

"She was bad, was she?"

"Bad is too nice a word. She was the tenant from hell. It started almost as soon as I gave her the keys. The constant stream of young men and the car doors slamming in the middle of the night. People running over the lawns shouting at two in the morning and then the incident with my precious cat, Lady."

"What happened?"

"She said that she was run over on the road, but I just knew that it was one of her fancy friends that did it. Well, as you can imagine, this was the straw that broke the donkey's back. I asked her to leave. When she refused, I waited until she went out and changed the lock."

"Was that the last time that you saw her?"

"I wish that it had been. She broke into the bungalow through the window with one of her thuggish boyfriends. They brought a van up to the front door, and loaded her stuff and some of mine into the back. That was the last I ever saw of her."

"Why didn't you call the police?"

"I would have done that night, but the bitch had cut the telephone wires. In the end, when I thought about it in the cold, clear light of dawn, I felt that the police were not such a good idea. With the sort of friends that she had, I would have always been looking over my shoulder."

"I take it that she didn't give you a forwarding address."

"Of course not. I wouldn't have wanted one either."

"What about the letter off the sponsor?"

"What about it?"

"Do you still have it?"

"Yes."

"Can I see it?"

He reached into the drawer underneath the coffee table and pulled out a box.

He handed me an envelope. "I hardly think that you are going to find the young lady there; otherwise, she would have lived there rather than here.

I had to admit that what he was saying was logical. I wrote down the address anyway.

To whom it may concern.

I can vouch for the honesty of Miss Breanna Holcomb

I am willing to be a guarantor for any debt that she may incur while living at your property.

Please find enclosed a bank statement.

I am the owner of the Good as New Second Hand Goods Store.

Yours sincerely,

Mr D Blake

12 Carlow Street

Altrincham

CHAPTER SIX

One of the places that I love the best in the entire world is my local pub, The Old One Hundred. If you work your way around all of the misinformation of how it got to be called such a strange name, you are left with an oasis for serious drinkers in a modern world of wine bars and corporate lounges.

The One Hundred could never be described as fashionable, but that is the reason why I love it so much. It is only a drunken stagger away from my apartment with a series of fish and chip shops, Chinese takeaways, and Indian Curry Houses along the way. What more can a man ask for? Plus, the aggressive vibe keeps away all of the students and trendies, who prefer more sedate drinking holes with less risk of winding up in hospital.

Shoddy was waiting for me in the bar and had already bought me a beer, which stood like an untouched beacon on the battered plywood table in front of his green leather chair.

Without my partner, I think it is safe to say that I would be doing another job. His brainpower and the ability to turn tedious routine work into a hobby left me free to get beaten up, shot at, and thrown through windows. We were the Stan Laurel and Oliver Hardy of private detectives.

I sat down, took a long drink, and went through my day. By the time I had finished, we were ready for another drink, and from then on, we hardly talked any business. When we arrived back home, he passed me an old newspaper cutting.

"This is the report on the dead body found in the pool. The press was determined to blame Fire as the person responsible. I would take a look at it before you go to bed."

By the time the old church clock across the road chimed midnight, I was tucked up in bed, scanning the crumpled brown stained newspaper from the 1960s. It made good reading and kept me awake. When the clock chimed one o'clock, I was fast asleep, and Shoddy was throwing a vodka party for one in the flat next door.

The next morning I was up early and, after some toast and tea, made my way to my dilapidated office situated in the High Street above a betting shop.

I telephoned Mercy Austin and told her that I would call around later that morning. She told me not to bother as Bruce Rush from Red Strip Entertainments was on his way over to my office. Her idea was for me to tell him everything. She didn't seem upset by the lack of news or the lack of her husband, but I put it down to her being in shock.

Bruce Rush was just a wet behind the ears pup and didn't look old enough to have a responsible job. He looked like he would have been more at home in the Lower Sixth chess club than running an agency that I assumed had to be big if it had Beasley Street as a client.

He was ghostly white with blonde hair and intense electric blue eyes. They had a faraway look that could have been drug-induced. I guessed that they weren't from my own personal experience of having an ex-drug addict as a partner.

"What you are telling me, Mr Shannon, is that Fire and Connor are still missing, and so is the money."

I didn't like the way he had summed up the situation. Maybe he wasn't as dumb as he looked. "That is the situation at the moment, but I am following a couple of leads."

"You know, of course, that we still haven't called the police, as we are now paying you a fee…"

"Plus expenses," I hastily added.

"As we are now paying you a fee plus limited expenses. What is your advice? Do you think that the police should be informed or not?"

I had picked up a copy of the free Croxley newspaper, and the murder of David Blake was front-page news. I held it up. "I assume that you have seen this, Bruce."

"Yes, I have. They don't have a name, but you do. Is this correct?"

"That is correct, Bruce. I am going to follow up on one of the leads after we finish our meeting, then I will report back to either you or Mercy Austin. What about Hilary Crash?"

"Hilary has taken it rather badly. She is with Mercy, but I would talk to Mercy." He added, "You will get more sense out of her."

"Can you give some more detail about the alleged murder incident involving Fire?"

"That was a long time ago. Is it relevant?"

"I don't know. It could be. Certainly, at the time it was big news. Naked body, rock star, swimming pool. The press must have enjoyed it."

"These sorts of things happen. It was before I was born. You probably know more about it than me."

"I know that it finished the band. They were forced to go to Germany. Could somebody have a grudge against Fire? You know that the body was never identified."

"Yes, I know all about that. I also know that it affected members of the band in different ways."

"Didn't Hilary Crash have a nervous breakdown?"

"Not because of any dead body. She had a serious drink problem and spent almost a year in a rehab unit in the USA. I believe she fully recovered and hasn't had a problem since."

"Yet, the band didn't try to make a comeback until now?"

"I think that they have to thank me for the comeback. They had split up and had all been doing other things. Not very successfully, I might add. It was very easy for me to persuade them to have another go. Fire was the problem. He had forged a very successful career for himself as a pop star. Without him in the line-up it would never have worked."

"How did you persuade him?"

"A little bit of playing to his ego, and then a lot playing to his greed. It seems that Fire always wanted to be a cult hero, and teenybop pop star to young American kids just didn't give him the buzz he required."

I looked at Bruce Rush with respect. He was a wolf in sheep's clothing—somebody not to mess with. I pushed my contract across the desk.

"By the way, I have only been hired on a verbal agreement to do the investigation. Do you want to sign the formal contract?"

Happily, he didn't hesitate. I countersigned and gave him a carbon copy.

CHAPTER SEVEN

I took the slip road off the M56 and joined a slow line of traffic moving towards the inevitable road works. The traffic lights on our side of the holdup seemed to be constantly on red, and I was well and truly hyped up as I finally picked up the A562, which took me past the plush Altrincham golf course and deposited me onto an even plusher Carlow Street.

This was a classy part of town, and the cars that lined the leafy suburban semi-sprawl as I curb crawled my way through it put my Riley Elf to shame. Like all rich places, the house owners chose to have names rather than numbers, and by the time I had reached the end, I still hadn't found number twelve.

I was about to go back and see if I had missed it when I saw that just like there are two sides to every argument, there were two sides to Carlow Street. The side that I had now entered looked slightly more jaded, and as I went further down what was turning into a very long street, the houses got more bohemian. I guess that this was the side for argumentative losers.

There was a builder's yard, an iffy looking second-hand car lot, and a wooden Methodist Assembly Hall with a broken cross on top along with the obligatory curry house and kebab joint.

The second-hand shop, As Good as New, had a hand-painted sign above the door and a space on either side where other buildings must have once stood. All that was left of those buildings was rubble. I wondered what they had been and how long it would be before the wrecking ball came for As Good as New.

A car horn blasted as I slowed down, and I was forced to pull up onto the narrow dirt hard shoulder. There was no other place to park, and I took an age trying to manoeuvre the Elf close enough to the wall so as not to block traffic. I eventually got fed up, got out, and crossed the road.

The shop window was filthy and had a crack running down its side from top to bottom. Several old guitars and banjos hung up on nails fixed to a plywood wall. The wall shielded the inside of the shop. The plywood was attached to the ceiling by two large hooks and swung slowly from side to side when an extra-large truck went by and hit a bump in the road.

In front of the musical instruments were diverse household goods, such as cigarette lighters and electrical appliances. They didn't seem to share a common theme, but what did I know? A large, old fashioned, none electric lawn mower took pride of place at the epicentre of the window. It had a sign on the wooden handle that explained that it could be mine for five pounds or equivalent item. I wondered what item would be equivalent to a lawnmower. Maybe a large pair of nail clippers, a vacuum cleaner, or a ukulele. Maybe all three.

I tried the door. It was locked even though the sign behind it said open.

I knocked on the glass and waited, then knocked some more. It was mornings like these that made me question my very reason for existing. I envied Shoddy and the life he led from the inside of a bottle.

A dim light came on somewhere at the back of the room, and I took advantage and knocked again on the frosted glass of the front door. I didn't do this too hard for fear of it shattering. Nothing about this shop lived up to its name. The small rectangle of glass was eventually filled by the shapely form of a woman. She called out from behind the door.

"We are not open on Wednesday."

I responded. "That's lucky for me. It's Tuesday."

She opened the door and peeped out at me through the crack she had created. Her face was pretty in a childish kind of way, and her dark eyes and poorly applied makeup gave her the look of somebody's little sister who had just been using big sister's blusher and mascara. I looked down and expected to see that she was wearing high heel shoes, three sizes too big. She was barefoot, and the rest of her body was definitely that of a mature woman.

She looked like she was about ready to burst into tears. "Are you selling something or buying?"

"Neither. I am looking for Breanna Holcomb. Can I assume that you are her?"

"You can assume what you want. Are you police?"

I showed her my ID card, and she read it intensely before handing it back. I waited for her to speak again. She was mulling over in her head whether to close the door on me, and I got ready to put my foot in the gap, which had been gradually getting bigger.

"I don't need to hire a Private Detective at the moment."

"I'm not selling my services. I want to speak to Breanna Holcomb on a matter of urgency."

"Has something happened to David?"

"Can I come in?"

"Are you sure that you are not the police?"

"Why? Have you been expecting them? Let me in, Breanna. I can't discuss this with you at the door."

She opened the door fully, and a bell on a spring above it clattered noisily. She locked it behind me as I stepped inside. The shop was tiny and cluttered with all sorts of stuff. A drum kit and an electric piano looked as if they had been in their allotted spaces for a long time.

Upstairs there was the sound of a radio and somebody walking around in stilettos. This, plus the constant drone of traffic, would have started to give me a headache if she hadn't shown me into a little living room at the back of the shop.

The room was neat and functional, though it lacked comfort and had no windows. There was a gas ring in the corner and an old-fashioned sink that was piled high with dishes. Several cups and mugs littered the table, and instead of a settee, there were two wooden chairs next to an empty fireplace. Above the fireplace, was a picture of a woman pushing a pram with two babies inside? I wondered who the babies were but didn't ask.

The room was lit by two very large strip lights, which gave it light, but zero ambience. It needed some kind of lamp. I wondered if

I had missed seeing one. I glanced around me but hadn't. The only other piece of furniture in the room was an ironing board covered with clothes waiting to be done. Funnily, there was no iron and no cupboard where she could have put it. There was something strange about Breanna; if this was actually her. I wondered if she was a natural blonde. She saw me looking and patted her permed hair into place.

"I hate this place, Mr Shannon. I hope to be moving on soon. Has something happened to David?"

"I was given your name by Harry Gittins. Do you remember him?"

She shrugged. "He was somebody I was acquainted with. I haven't seen him for years. Is this to do with him?"

"No, this is to do with David Blake. You got him a job with Harry Gittins. Is that correct?"

"I mentioned that David was looking for a job. He took him on, but that was his decision, not mine."

"Gittins also fired him from that job for gross misconduct. What do you know about that?"

"That's his word against David's. Personally, I would believe David."

"Is David, your boyfriend?"

"Not that it's your business, but no, he isn't."

"Would you mind telling me what your relationship is?"

"That's between him and me."

By the way, she was talking; she didn't seem to think he was dead. I didn't want it to be me that told her. She looked emotionally charged enough to do anything if I did, and if she chose to do something to herself, I didn't want that on my conscience. "Where are you from, Breanna?"

"You ask a lot of questions, Mr Shannon. I haven't done anything wrong, so why should I tell you anything?" Her voice softened a bit. "Have you any news about David? I have been worried?"

"When was the last time that you saw him?"

"A couple of weeks ago. He has a habit of doing that. But he would have normally called before now."

"Had he been acting strange?"

" Do you mean has he been up to his old tricks?"

"What tricks are those?"

"You're the detective. What is this about?"

"I am acting on behalf of a client. A serious crime has been committed, and David's name has been brought up. Other than this, I can't tell you anything. But you are quite within your rights to contact the police and ask about him."

"Meaning, he has been arrested."

"Look, Breanna, I don't think that it is up to me to do the work of the police. All I want to know is some background information on David Blake. If you are not prepared to give this to me, or you don't know anything, then I will be on my way."

"You know that he served nine years in prison?"

"I didn't. What for?"

"You had better ask him."

"How long has he been out?"

"A couple of years, and yes, he has been acting rather strange recently."

"What do you mean?"

"Nine years inside prison can do a lot of harm. He is obsessed and recently even more than before."

"With what?"

"An obsession with finding the person who wrongly put him there."

CHAPTER EIGHT

Shoddy was frying bacon in a skillet when I got back to his flat. He threw in some eggs and put in some bread to soak up the fat. As we ate and drank strong Yorkshire tea, I filled him in on my excursion to Altrincham.

"You never told her that David Blake was dead?"

"I already explained to you that I didn't want the responsibility. How was I to know what type of relationship she had with the guy? They may not have even been close. If they were very close, what if she tried to kill herself?"

Shoddy lit up a cigarette and continued eating. He opened a can of cider and drank it along with his tea. "The only information that we got off Breanna Holcomb was that David Blake had been in prison."

"For a crime that he didn't do," I added.

"Yeah, they all say that. Do you know which prison?"

"No."

"It shouldn't be too difficult to find out, as long as David Blake is his real name. I didn't show you this, did I?" He went into a box that was next to his chair and brought out a wallet. The one that I had taken out of Blake's coat. "You will never make a detective, Moggs. You missed this, though to be fair, so did I almost." He opened the wallet and prised apart a small, nearly invisible cut in the leather above the stitching. I thought it was a rip, but it turned out to be a credit card slot. Shoddy pulled out a small newspaper cutting and handed it to me.

It was a picture of a young-looking Beasley Street posing for photos in front of a crowd of photographers. The headline read, *Beasley Street begin a new major tour of Britain*

The picture could have been from any newspaper. It featured all four members, with Fire standing out in front and signing an autograph. "Maybe David Blake was a fan, Shod."

"Yeah. A fan of kidnapping and extorting money. I've met people like him before. Kidnapping is a crime done by specialists. They very rarely end up good for anybody, especially the victim. Who knows, this time it could have also ended up badly for Beasley Street. With Blake gone, how do we know where Crash and Fire are?"

"Somebody has to know."

"I hope you're right. I reckon that David Blake's accomplish decided that the money was not enough to share. Could the killer have also gone back and finished off Crash and Fire?"

"Maybe."

"Do you think that Breanna Holcomb could have the bottle to kill somebody with a knife?"

"My gut feeling is no, but when have I ever been right."

"I think this case is already too big for us. Has Mercy Austin phoned the police yet?"

"I don't know."

"Well, maybe you should phone her up and tell her to. The police are stumped; at least they would then have a motive for the murder."

Shod, as always, was right. I picked up the phone and dialled Mercy Austin. The phone was picked up after a longish wait, and the person on the other end said in a cheerful voice that I was through to Hilary Crash. She sounded too happy for somebody whose husband had just been kidnapped. She also sounded a bit drunk.

"This is Morris Shannon here, Hilary. Is it possible to speak to Mercy?"

She laughed hollowly. "Am I not good enough to speak to, Mr Shannon?"

"Yes, you or Mercy will do. All that I wanted to say was that I think you should now call the police."

"Is that your professional advice?"

"Er, yeah, it is. I strongly advise it."

"Do you want my opinion?"

"Of course, Hilary."

"My opinion is that we don't need to do anything."

"And why is that?"

"Because Fire and Connor strolled into the house a couple of hours ago. They had been to a farmhouse in Scotland to finish the mix of the new album. Apparently, it was Connor's idea. He said that they needed absolute tranquillity, which of course, they couldn't get here with all the press interest. The four of them are in the studio now listening to the results and planning their first tour."

"Does Fire know about the money he has lost?

"Not yet. Do you want to come over and tell him? After all, you are still, technically, our security guard."

CHAPTER NINE

The book hit the mantelpiece and fell onto the hearth. I wondered if it was going to start to burn or just smoulder. I had just told Fire about the kidnapping fiasco and the fact that one hundred thousand pounds of his money was now missing.

If this was how rock stars carried on when they had bad news, I was willing to believe all of the stuff I had read in the newspapers about them driving cars into swimming pools and wrecking hotel rooms. He lifted up a tray with fresh coffee on it. He looked at the pristine white wall in front of him and decided against it. Maybe age was starting to catch up with him, or just maybe he was worried about what his wife would say.

He put the tray down and poured us both a cup of coffee.

"What's the chance of me getting my money back?"

"It's a possibility."

"How much of a possibility?"

"I would need to check a few leads out before I could tell you that."

He took a sip of coffee and thought about it. "If I hire you to investigate this, are you saying that there is no guarantee of success?"

"I would say that I have a better chance than if you go to the police. Plus, if you did, then they would want to know why you didn't contact them before."

"Before?"

"Well, police are a bit funny when dead bodies turn up on their patch, and there are no clues as to who committed the murder."

"Oh, you mean the man that sent Mercy the note."

"Yes, that's the one. His name was David Blake. Does it ring any bells?"

He shook his head. "How did this man know that we had gone away?"

"Now that is the big question. If I could answer that, then I think I would be a lot closer to getting your money back."

"Do this for me, Morris, and there will be a nice juicy bonus."

"Tell me about the body in the swimming pool?"

If he was phased by my question, he didn't look it.

"Nothing to tell, Morris. You know how it is."

"Not really. Tell me how it is."

"When you are famous and making a lot of money, you have a lot of hangers-on. That was the case with Beasley Street back then. We were a lot younger, and when we threw a party, I could guarantee that I didn't know fifty percent of the people that came. All I remember about the whole affair is getting a bit intoxicated and passing out. When I woke up, the police were swarming through the house, and I was being arrested."

"You didn't know the boy?"

"No."

"Did any member of the band know him?"

"No, or at least they didn't say."

"But you weren't formally charged."

"No, Mercy got a top lawyer down to the police station, and I was out within an hour or so. They didn't have a case against me. Just because I was by the pool didn't mean that I had a hand in killing him."

"Somebody hit him over the head. Did you see anything?"

"No. The police never found his clothes, and to this day, they don't know who he was."

"I believe that you did not get much support off the press."

"They were horrible to us. That's what the journalists are like in this country. They build you up just to knock you down. And what a good job they did. Every day for weeks, they said that because we were rich and famous, we thought that we could get away with murder. Of course, it destroyed our career. Hilary had a nervous breakdown and ended up in a clinic in America, and we headed into permanent exile in Germany. We split up soon after that, but I managed to get work in the USA and built my career back as a solo artist. I never forgot the band, though."

"Why did you get back together?"

"Let's just say it was unfinished business. We could be even more successful now than we were back then. Only…"

"Only?"

"Only we don't need another body, Morris. That would screw things up, and there would be no third comeback. That's why I want you to go about your business and get me that money back. We don't need any police involvement."

"Why did you go away and not tell anybody?"

"That was Connor's idea. He knew that I had a house in Scotland, and we were joking about in the studio wondering how long it would take us to finish mixing the album. We were getting constantly interrupted. Connor said why don't we go up to the house and take a couple of hours without telephones. He was right; we finished the whole thing in a day."

"But, you were away for two days."

"We took advantage of the river in my garden and went salmon fishing."

"Why didn't you tell your wives?"

"Because they would have wanted to come and would not have stopped phoning. Besides, Mercy was used to me disappearing. I didn't think she would be worried.

It was a weird situation, but the way he told it sounded right. Connor Crash was asleep, and Mercy Austin was at the beautician's, but I took advantage of Hilary Crash's presence as I made my way out. She was making coffee in the kitchen.

She didn't ask, just put another cup on the table in front of me and poured. I declined milk and sugar and sat down.

"Did he ask you?" She sat down and lit a small black cigarillo, which smelt quite nice even to my smoke sensitive nose.

"Ask me what?"

"Fire is panicking. I do believe that he will be wiped out if you don't get him his money back."

"That sort of money is a lot to lose."

"He's had more. That's more than Connor or any of the other lads have ever had."

"Do I detect a hint of jealousy, Mrs Crash?"

"I'm not jealous of anybody, and please don't call me that. I'm Hilary."

"Ok, Hilary, I'll rephrase it. Do you think that he doesn't deserve to have made a career for himself as a solo artist?"

"That's what happens with singers. In the end, they don't need a band; they just need a bunch of session musicians playing the music. It has never changed. Never will. He's not the only one panicking. The others have got more to lose."

"I don't understand."

"They don't need another body. The last one wrecked what should have been a great career. Forget the money that Fire has lost. This comeback by the band will turn that into peanuts."

"Yeah, I get it, but it doesn't stop Fire from trying to recover the money."

"Whoever stole it will be long gone by now."

"I was coming to that, Hilary. Do you have any ideas who could have written the note?"

"Not a clue, I'm afraid."

"He told me that only he and Connor knew about going to Scotland. Did Connor tell you?"

"Connor wouldn't tell me anything if Fire told him not to."

"That sounds a bit strange. You are, after all, husband and wife. Shouldn't you share everything?"

"You have never been in a band, Morris. It's all about lads bonding. I'm just a wife; they are the band. What they share is much more important than marriage."

"You sound bitter."

"You sound desperate for a lead. I'm sorry, but if you are looking for a band member to have stolen Fire's money, then you are looking in the wrong place."

"What about the last body? The one in the swimming pool."

"What about it? Do you think the two bodies are connected?"

"Maybe. How come nobody at the party recognised him?"

"You must have been told why. Back in those days, we used to get loads of gate crashers."

"Yeah, but not dead ones."

"What about the Rolling Stones?"

"Who?"

"Morris, you can't tell me that you have never heard of the Rolling Stones?"

"Vaguely, Rolling Stone does ring a bell. What about him?"

"They were a band, Morris, not a person. Their guitarist, Brian Jones, was found dead in a swimming pool. These things happen. Funny, it didn't seem to affect their career."

"How did the body in the pool affect you, Hilary? I heard that you had a nervous breakdown and spent a year in a clinic in America."

"Oh yeah, there was that. In those days, there weren't many rehab clinics in the States. It wasn't depression brought on by any dead body. I was an alcoholic, and I realised that I needed to sort myself out. We all knew that things were about to change, and for me, it gave me a chance to clean myself up. I went to the Betty Ford Clinic in California. I was there for months. The band went to Europe and then pretty quickly split up. Everybody did different things. They all hated Fire."

"Why?"

"Because he got himself a new deal and made loads of money. He got himself a new band and forgot about us."

"What did you all do?"

"Connor carried on playing on the continent. There was plenty of work for British musicians in Germany and Holland, but it was long hours and low pay. Buddy Fox, the drummer, did the same, and Greg Angel went back to his old job."

"What was that?"

"He was a bricklayer. He also stayed out in Germany."

"And now you are all back together."

"Yes. Twenty years down the line and we have a second chance, and we've still got a dead body hanging around our necks."

"A different body."

"A body is a body, Morris. It's not great publicity."

"Was it Bruce Rush that got you back together?"

"Yes, he is only young, but he certainly did the work and brought them together again. He even convinced Fire that his best days could still be ahead of him."

"Yes, Fire must have been the most difficult to convince."

"Why do you say that, Morris?"

"Because of his big solo career."

"Don't you believe it. He wanted this as badly as all of the others. His career was practically washed up. That house he has got in Scotland has been up for sale for a year. Nobody wants to buy it. Beasley Street was the rescue package. I bet he wishes that he hadn't been so secretive about skiving off to his mansion in Scotland. That was a very expensive couple of days."

CHAPTER TEN

"Have you got any ideas, Shod, or have we hit a brick wall?"

We were sitting in the bar of the One Hundred trying to work out our next move.

"It could have been anyone, Moggs."

"Yeah, I know that, but we need to at least narrow it down."

"I've got bits of nothing, which I've gathered. We could start there. At least we will be earning our money."

"What have you got?"

"Like I said, nothing much, but that's all we have. I checked out David Blake."

"And?"

"And, I got a name. Blake went to Wakefield prison, but if you want to know why you will have to go there and see this bloke." He handed me a piece of paper with the name Forest Moore written on it. "These old police records are stored separately on microfiche. You will need to go and look for yourself."

"All the way to Wakefield?"

"Either that or we give the money back."

"I'll do it tomorrow. It will be a nice run out for the Elf."

"Oh yeah, and there was one other thing. That newspaper cutting that I found."

"What about it?"

He went into his coat pocket, brought it out, and handed it to me.

"Look carefully. What can you see?"

"Just the band signing autographs."

He sighed. "You will never make a detective, mate. There are two clues on this small newspaper cutting."

"Can't you just tell me?"

"One is obvious, and the other a bit less."

"I guess that means no."

"Moggsy, you need to start thinking for yourself."

"Why, when I have you to think for me."

"OK; take a look at the man signing the autograph."

"I am, but I can't see anything."

Shoddy drained his glass and waited for me to drain mine. He got up and walked towards the bar. "I expect you to have found at least one of the clues by the time I get back. What do I always tell you about detective work?"

"It's about detail."

"That's right." He went into his pocket and dropped a magnifying glass on my lap. While he was buying the beer, I scanned the picture closely. By the time he got back, I needed a drink, but I still hadn't found anything."

"Shoddy sat down and took a sip of beer. " Give Up?"

"You make it sound like a children's game, Shod, and yes, put me out of my misery."

"Take a close look at the girl getting her autograph book signed."

I placed the magnifying glass over her face, and I saw who it was.

"That's a very young-looking Hilary Crash."

"And look where the band was."

"There is no sign saying anything like that, mate. It could have been anywhere."

"Look again, Sherlock: bottom left."

"It's just an advert for kitchen tiles. All newspapers have them. What has that got to do with Hilary Crash and Beasley Street?"

I could tell that Shoddy was getting irritated by the way he drained his beer and handed me the empty glass.

"Read the advert."

"It says deluxe kitchen tiles are half price for one week only. Check out the giveaway prices at the tile warehouse."

"And the address?"

"Giselle Terrace… Wakefield."

"Looks like we have a West Yorkshire connection. It could be nothing, but it's worth taking a look. Get the beers in, and I'll tell you what you need to do tomorrow."

CHAPTER ELEVEN

Forest Moore was sitting in a miserable looking cubicle in the foyer of a nameless grey building on the outskirts of Wakefield. He was filling in a pile of light green forms and biting his nails at the same time. Even from a distance, I could see that this thin, balding, middle-aged man was almost exploding with pent up nervous energy.

His washed-out, grey eyes picked me up as I knocked on the cubicle window, and he threw down his pen and opened it grudgingly. He took a swig of some brown liquid from a cup at the side of his desk and visibly winced.

"No sugar," he proclaimed. "The story of my life," he added.

"Mr Moore?"

"That will be me. And if I'm not wrong, you must be Morris Shannon."

I admitted that I was and out of politeness asked him how he had known.

"Shoddy said that you were six feet four with a bald head. We don't get many in that look like that. Well, in fact, we don't get any. How is Shoddy?"

"The usual."

"Ah, better not say anymore. I'm surprised that he has lived so long, but probably fitter than the two of us for all the amount of drink he consumes."

"Did he tell you what I want?"

"He did. The stuff you were asking about is so old that it is stored on microfiche. Have you ever used a microfiche machine?"

"No."

"Not to worry, it's not rocket science. All you need to do is put the plastic sheet under the lens and then scroll through to what you want. There is a button to make the file bigger."

"There is no paper police file for me to look at?"

"No. That would have been incinerated years ago. The Yorkshire Police have been going all technical. Storing files on plastic takes up less space and reduces the dust. Don't worry, as an ex-serving police officer; I used to love the smell and touch of a case file. I know exactly how you feel about all of these changes. Those microfiche machines have no soul. You know, back in the days when I was a cop, I reckon I could smell a clue from a case file or an old black and white mug-shot."

"You used to be a cop?"

"Twenty-five years on the force man and boy; most of that as a detective sergeant."

"Where did you serve?"

"Here, lad. I spent most of my time in Wakefield. I knew all of the low-life and scum that inhabit the streets around here. Still do, as a matter of fact. Back in the old days, it was much better than it is now. Criminals knew their place. If you nicked them, they would usually come quietly. These days they are all tooled up. Some carry guns and most have knives. No, I would not want to be starting off in the force these days."

"How come you got this job?"

"Records? Somebody had to do it. I asked, and I got the nod."

As he spoke, he closed the window and locked it. He came out of a side door and beckoned me to follow him to a lift at the side of the cubicle. We entered together, and he pressed basement.

"The bowels of hell, Morris. There are no windows. You're not claustrophobic, are you?"

"I'll let you know in half an hour."

The lift bumped to a halt, and we got out into a large room with several strange-looking machines against the far wall. There were filing cabinets against the other two. The air had a plastic smell about it.

"What was the name of the case you wanted to look at?"

"David Blake. He was sent down for at least nine years. About eleven years ago."

"I was still a cop, then. I think that is when I first met your partner, Shoddy. It was on a course about money laundering, and those nights in the bar were legendary. He certainly could knock the beer and whisky back. No, wait a minute, that must have been fifteen years ago. Doesn't time fly, Morris?"

I agreed that it did and sat patiently by a machine while he hunted for the file. It was a bit of an anti-climax when he came back holding a piece of plastic, which he placed in the machine. He looked at the screen, turned a large wheel at the side, and brought up an image that was headed, David Blake,

"All of the stuff that you need will be on this. Turn the wheel to go backwards and forwards and this little green wheel for focus, and if you need to enlarge it." He glanced at his watch. "I'm off on a break now; I will be back in a bit. If anybody comes down, just say that you are doing a job for Forest Moore. Have fun."

There was a picture of a young-looking David Blake minus the knife in his neck. He was a plain-looking youth with a face carrying an arrogant and menacing expression and acne. The file that followed went into detail about a warehouse robbery and the attempted theft of twenty thousand packets of cigarettes. The report was badly written and was not what you would have called in depth.

From what I gathered, there was a vicious attack on one of the security guards, and he was severely injured.

Statements from two other guards confirm that they were jumped by at least four masked intruders, tied up, and locked in their own office. The guard who was injured had been doing an inspection round of the warehouse. He had been beaten about the head with a blunt instrument, which was thought to have been a baseball bat.

I scrolled down, and there was not much more information. There were statements from several witnesses, which included a milkman and a drunk. The drunk had been sleeping in a nearby shop doorway.

The robbery had taken place in May and seemed to have been a complete success. None of the gang members had been caught, and there were no clues about who they were. The general feeling was that they were from out of town.

Following the report were lots of pictures taken at the scene of the crime. There were almost a hundred of these, and they told me nothing.

The machine was slow and went in and out of focus at will. I had been in there for almost an hour and found out nothing. Finally, the warehouse images finished, and I came to a statement that was headed Christine Finn.

The statement was short and was also typed out. Christine Finn said that she was the live-in girlfriend of David Blake. She also stated that there were thousands of packets of cigarettes stored in a cellar. She also claimed that when she asked where the cigarettes had come from, David Blake had become aggressive and beaten her up.

I searched for something else, but the microfiche ended there. I wondered if there was another piece of plastic, and was relieved when I heard the lift mechanism spring into life.

"Everything all right?" Forrest smelt of cheese and onion and had traces of tomato ketchup on his top lip.

"This file ended a bit abruptly. I was expecting something about the arrest and the trial."

"These are police case files, Morris, not books by Agatha Christie."

"I realise that, Forest, but I would have expected a conclusion."

"That's all a bit too political for me, Morris. When they did the conversions, it was all a bit of a rush. Some of the older files did not convert very well."

"I don't understand."

"It's simple, Morris. Some of the old files had been stored in very damp conditions. There was a flood in the mid-nineteen-seventies, and a lot of them were water-damaged. They salvaged what they could. To be honest, you are the first person that has been down here this year. It is not the sort of thing that gets looked at much."

"It looks like I have wasted a journey."

"Let me have a look." He scrolled through the file quickly and stopped at the statement from Christine Finn. "Are you interested in one of the Finns?"

"I'm not sure, Forrest. Who are they?"

"A bad lot. I know or rather knew them very well. I was a young cop on the Eastmoor Estate patrol. The Finn family were notorious. Small-time stuff, but they were persistent."

"Do you know this case?"

"David Blake? Nope, never heard of him. I would have been promoted by then. I was transferred to Doncaster. Lost track of all my contacts in Wakefield for a couple of years, and then I came back."

"So, you can't tell me anything?"

"I can tell you that we have lost half of the file. It was probably burned years ago."

"What do you suggest that I do now?"

"Well, you could try the Finns, but if you are going onto the Eastmoor Estate, I would keep an eye on your car, and don't go after dark."

CHAPTER TWELVE

Forest Moore was right about the Eastmoor estate, but I had a lot of confidence that even a hardened car thief would draw the line about stealing a Riley Elf. As the doors didn't lock, I had no alternative but to trust in my awful taste in motors.

I had stopped at a telephone box on my way over to look for the Finn family's address. There were only three Finns listed and just the one with an address on Eastmoor. The name of the street was also Eastmoor, and the number was two, so I didn't have to write it down.

The council house looked well kept, and though it only had a small garden, it had a freshly mowed lawn and a crazy pavement path. Parked up near the front door was a powerful looking motorbike, and the front window displayed a Vote Labour sign, with the picture of a smiling politician.

The lady who answered the door was friendly enough and hardly glanced at my ID before letting me in. She led me through into the combined kitchen and living room, which smelt of sour milk and air freshener.

She looked like she was in her mid-fifties and was attractive if you liked an overly made up and dyed blonde hair vibe.

I joined her on the settee, and she adjusted her light blue jeans, which looked at least a size too small. "Make this quick; love. I am off to bingo in a minute, and the taxi charges for waiting."

"I have come about your daughter, Christine."

"Why, what has she been up to?"

"No, nothing like that. I was wondering if she was in, or if you have a forwarding address?"

"No to both of those. What's this about?"

"It's about a serious crime, Mrs Finn, that has been committed in Liverpool…"

"That's a bit formal, Love; Call me Elsie. Did she commit it? I know that she can't resist getting into trouble." She reached over to her handbag, brought out a packet of cigarettes, and lit one. "Takes after her father. Murdered somebody, has she?"

"No, she hasn't. I don't want to talk to her about something that she has done. I want some information."

"Information? You are not going to get anything out of that one. Besides, I haven't got a clue where she is. She only turns up when she wants something. She gets that off her father as well."

"She gave a statement to the police about fifteen years ago. It was about her boyfriend. His name was David Blake. Do you know him?"

"If I did, then I can't remember. Man mad was our Chrissie. She went through them as I go through packets of cigarettes. I think it was a lack of a male influence in the house. Her father, God rest his soul, was inside prison more than he was out. No, Chrissie was a lethal combination. Her father was not the brightest lamp in the street, but she inherited his thieving lying personality and my brains."

"Have you got an address where I can reach her, Elsie?"

"No."

"Could you telephone her and ask if she will meet with me?"

"I don't think that you understand, Love. I have lost contact with her. She lived a secretive life while she was under this roof. Now that she isn't, she could be anywhere. Knowing her, she might not even be in the country."

"And you don't know anything about a David Blake being sent down for grievous bodily harm?"

"What did he do?"

"He robbed a warehouse and, allegedly, attacked a night watchman."

"And Chrissie?"

"She gave a statement to the police about him."

"You're living in fantasy land, Love. Whatever she is, she is still a Finn. We would never grass anybody to the police. I think that you have got that all wrong."

"And David Blake? Are you saying that name doesn't ring a bell?"

She made an exaggerated face to look as if she was thinking deeply. "Yes, I think that is exactly what I am saying, and now if you don't mind, Mr Private Detective, I've got a game of bingo with my name written on it to play."

CHAPTER THIRTEEN

The journey back from Wakefield seemed to take treble the time it had taken me to get there. In the end, it had been a wasted trip, but I did have a couple of names that I didn't have before. The Finn family could prove to fit in somewhere. They seemed to have the right sort of reputation, though without finding the whereabouts of Christine Finn, I could not make much progress.

The A642 was a beast of a road that snaked out in front of me with potential death waiting around every sharp curve. By the time it arrived at the A62 motorway and deposited me near the brass band town of Brighouse, my nerves were well and truly shot to pieces, and the rain had turned to heavy sleet, and then snow.

The motorway had other dangers as wall-to-wall cars sped to their destinations, completely ignoring that the road's grey mantle was becoming whiter by the minute. By the time I reached sleepy Rochdale, the snow had once again turned to rain, and as I flew past Manchester Airport, the night had got bored with the stormy conditions and left me alone under a billion stars and a bright three-quarter moon. The traffic seemed to have been dissolved by the weather conditions, and I had become undecided about my next move.

I had the choice between the road home and the road to Litherland and the house owned by Beasley Street. Reluctantly I chose Litherland. Murder and robbery were reasons enough not to want to go to bed, but I also was unsure if I should still be acting as security, and should be sleeping metaphorically with the band.

My headlights picked up the brilliant whitewashed wall of number twelve Lightfoot Street, and I saw that there was somebody at home. There was a black Ford of some description parked on the gravel near the door. I slid my Riley Elf next to it. Bruce Rush answered the door. He looked even younger than the last time I had seen him, and did I detect some slight embarrassment in his manner?

His eyes looked tired, but I suspected that this was alcohol-induced. This was confirmed when I caught a whiff of his breath. It was flavoured with either whisky or brandy. He certainly didn't look like a beer drinker. He looked more like he should be curled up in bed with some hot chocolate and biscuits.

He didn't seem to want to let me in, though he did maintain an inane smile as he blocked my entrance.

"It's rather late for social visits, Mr Shannon. Has something important happened? Have you found the money or solved the murder?"

"No, not yet. I was hoping to have a quiet word. I have made some progress, and I guessed that you would be interested to see that I was earning my money."

"The band is not here. That's what musicians are like. They have been gone all day. Practicing for their national tour." He looked at his watch. "These old-timers are very keen. Not like the young bands of today. These guys are perfectionists and will probably be at it all night. I don't know how they can keep it up."

"It was either Mercy or Hilary that I wanted to see. Are they in?"

"Mercy is with her husband. I'm afraid that the only one at home is Hilary."

"That must be cosy."

He narrowed his eyes, and I realised that it had come out wrong.

"What are you implying? I don't like riddles, Mr Shannon."

"Look, son, I'm not talking in riddles; I'm just tired and have had a long day. Are you going to let me in or not?"

"If you put it that way, then I suppose you had better come in," he said sullenly. He added, "I'm not paying you overtime, though."

"That's very mean of you, Bruce," said Hilary Crash from a doorway at the end of the hall. "If you find Fire's money, then I think that a bonus would be well deserved. Of course, the murder of that awful man is of little importance. One less deviant in the world is a good thing, don't you think, Mr Shannon?"

"A murder is a murder," was a pretty lame reply, but was all that I had. "Can I come in and sit down, or are we going to talk out here?"

"Of course, forgive Bruce for his inhospitality, Mr Shannon. Come through and tell me all of the news."

She directed me to an armchair by the open fireplace. The fact that all of the cushions on the settee opposite were crumpled was not wasted on me. It looked like Hillary and Bruce were pretty close. I wondered how close and if it was relevant.

Birch logs were burning low in the grate, and the room had that comfy wood smoke smell about it that would have sent me to sleep had I been allowed to close my eyes for a couple of minutes. In the background, there was orchestral music playing. Obviously, one of them was not a fan of beat music, and I couldn't blame them because neither was I.

"What do you want to drink, Mr Shannon? Bruce will be the barman."

"Whisky?" I asked, hopefully.

"Off you go, Bruce, and make it a big one. Mr Shannon looks as tired as I feel."

She sat down on the settee, fluffed all of the cushions into shape, and rearranged them. Was she aware that I was aware? Probably, but it was none of my business. I had heard what goes on in the music industry.

Satisfied, she placed another log on the fire. "I do like a nice fire, don't you, Mr Shannon."

"Yeah, terrific."

"Tell me what you've got."

"I've been up to Wakefield today."

"Really. And why was that?"

"The man that was murdered was a convicted armed robber. He went to Wakefield prison and could have possibly come from there."

"Fascinating. And did you get any clues? Is that what you detectives call them?"

"I hit a blank in many ways, but maybe you can help me. Aren't you originally from Wakefield?"

"Why would you say that? That's in Yorkshire, isn't it?"

I fumbled in my pocket and brought out the old picture that I had got from David Blake's wallet. "Isn't this you in the picture?"

"Yes. It looks that way."

"That picture was taken by the local newspaper in Wakefield."

"Then, I must have been there. I probably went there to see the band. I did that in those days."

"Just for the record, Hilary, where are you from?"

"Sheffield. Have you been there?"

"No."

"I think that Bruce has gone there to get you that drink. Shall I go and get you one myself?"

I was feeling very tired now. The heat of the room was sapping the energy levels out of my head. I got up. "No, I think I need bed more than alcohol." I headed for the door. "Just one last thing. Does the name Finn ring any bells?"

"I don't think so, Mr Shannon, but if any of the boys know the name, I will let you know."

CHAPTER FOURTEEN

When I got back home, I knocked on Shoddy's door as I passed to get to my flat.

"It's open," he shouted.

He was sitting in his favourite armchair watching TV. There was a longhaired band playing loud rock music, and I was surprised that he hadn't switched channels.

I got myself a beer and sat on the settee.

"BBC documentary. Don't you recognise them?"

I looked more closely. It was Beasley Street in their heyday. It cut to a picture of an older version of the band lounging around the pool at the house in Lightfoot Street. Connor Crash was in a pair of Speedos and seemed oblivious to his big beer gut. Hilary was sitting next to him and was doing all of the talking about the big plans that they had.

Shoddy got up and went over to the fridge to get himself a beer. He brought a bottle of whisky and a couple of glasses from the sideboard. He poured us both two generous shots and settled himself back down.

"It's been on for about an hour. It should be finished in a minute, which is a relief. They weren't that good and are even worse now."

As the titles went up the screen, the last few shots were of the band in the recording studio where I had first met them. I had to admit that Shoddy was right. As musical entertainment, I preferred German military music. At least it was played by people with sensible haircuts.

Shoddy seemed pleased with himself. "I've been doing some checking."

"Well done, Shod."

"No need to be sarcastic. It's the checking part of the job that makes your work easy."

"What have you come up with?"

"I've got this for a start." He handed me a photograph of a young man floating face up in a swimming pool. He looked vaguely familiar. "That's the mysterious body that nobody can identify."

"Did you identify him?"

"No, I'm not that good, Moggs, but I did dig up a couple of facts on the band."

"Go on."

"Firstly, did you know that Fire was charged with assault but got off with a suspended sentence? It was under his real name of Ford Austin."

"Who did he assault?"

"Connor Crash."

"Why did he do that?"

"It was heard in the magistrate's court, so it's not very clear as to why. You never get to the truth when a magistrate is involved. Fire claimed it was self-defence. Neither man would go into detail about what the argument was about, but do you want to know what I think?"

"What do you think, Shod?"

"I reckon it was about a woman."

"Any particular woman in mind?"

"Probably either Hilary Crash or Mercy Austin. Either way, it seems that Connor has a bit of a temper. But from watching that documentary, it looks like Fire is a bit of a creep."

"Anything else?"

"Not for now, but it might be a good idea for you to go back and see Breanna Holcomb, but this time take the picture. If David Blake carried it around in his wallet, then maybe he might have told her the reason why."

"Isn't it obvious?"

"Not to me."

"He carried it around because he was going to kidnap one of them."

"The picture is at least twenty-years-old. He couldn't have been planning it for that long. I'm just saying that a visit might be a good idea. Have you got anything else to do tomorrow morning?"

"No."

He poured us both another couple of shots. "While you're doing that, I'll do a bit more digging. Oh yeah, I almost forgot. Hilary Crash didn't spend any time in rehab in the States."

"How can you be so sure, Shod?"

"Because there was nobody of that name in the Betty Ford Clinic in Rancho Mirage California. This is either as an outpatient or an inmate."

"Maybe she got the name wrong, and it was someplace else."

"Or maybe she was doing something else?"

"Such as what?"

Shoddy put his coat on and headed for the door. "That is something that I haven't worked out yet. If we rush, we can get to the pub before it closes. We'll sort it all out tomorrow."

CHAPTER FIFTEEN

I hated the early morning traffic in the Croxley town centre and usually did my best to avoid it by staying in bed. Out of a sense of trying to give value for money, I had got out of bed early, had a cup of tea and some toast, and joined the angry commuters heading to their mind-numbing jobs. Already tempers were frayed, and as usual, it was the women who were the worse. I reckoned it was the school run and this was confirmed when a fat old bird still wearing curlers, cut me up and shook her fist in my general direction even though I had done nothing wrong.

My sense of injustice became heightened when her three daughters, on the back seat, looked out of the rear window and pulled their tongues out. Don't you just love rush hour?

There was a mustard coloured Mercedes parked by the wall on the other side of the second-hand shop. The driver was making a statement again and forcing me to squeeze into a space between a couple of wheelie bins and a rubbish skip. I didn't need to search my memory to remember where I had seen the wheels before. The door of the shop was closed, but there was an open sign behind the window. That seemed to be the only thing behind it as the shop looked glaringly empty.

I opened the door a bit, put my hand around the top, and grasped the bell. I entered silently and could have walked away with a drum kit or a Zulu spear and shield without anybody noticing. Certainly not the two people in the room behind the counter. The door was slightly open, but the conversation was heated enough for me to have heard even if it had been closed.

The man was doing most of the talking. I recognised his voice as the smooth-talking insurance salesman, Harry Gittins. Whatever he was doing here, it wasn't to sell Breanna a double indemnity policy, but I guessed that he had sold a few before he had arrived, judging by the car he was driving.

"It's not worth the risk, Breanna, for that sort of money. What would you be doing? Sitting here doing nothing and getting more than me."

"Beggars can't be choosers, H, I got the information, and all you have to do is pick up the money. It's sweet. You've done worse before for less."

"It's nowhere near enough."

"I found her. All you need to do is grab the booty."

"And if I get caught, they are going to put me inside and throw away the key."

"Don't exaggerate. Besides, it's money that has been stolen. What are they going to do? Go to the police?"

"Ask David Blake that. They didn't go to the police when he had the money. They found a permanent solution. A knife where it hurts."

"She doesn't know you. And you're a man."

"I'm glad you noticed, but wasn't David Blake also a man. It didn't seem to stop them from killing him."

"I'll give you another five thousand, but that's my final offer."

"No. I am taking a risk, and you are not even sure that it's her."

"It's her, alright. It has to be."

"And look at what happens to people that make her angry."

"Another ten thousand."

"I tell you, Breanna, it is still no." He added. "After all, I am a respectable businessman."

"Don't you mean a rip-off merchant?"

"Steady. I don't need to take this. I've got enough cash. Business has been good recently, so I don't need all this."

"Don't tell me that. How long have we known each other?"

"Long enough."

"Have I ever let you down?"

"Well, no."

"It's money for old rope. And besides, how do I know that I can trust you. You could make off with the whole hundred thousand."

"I have got a business to run. Where would I go? What would my wife say?"

"That's right, H, I trust you. Lean on the old bird, take the money, and we can share it eighty-twenty."

"Fifty, fifty."

"Sixty forty, and that's my last offer. Just think; you could get yourself a decent car with forty thousand."

"I've got a decent car if you haven't noticed."

"It's a poser's car. Get yourself something more in keeping with your role as a businessman like a Jaguar or a BMW."

"The Mercedes used to impress you. You called it the babe magnet."

"Sixty, forty, Harry. Do we have a deal?"

I heard him sigh. "Where do I find this woman?"

"She's in Liverpool. I saw her last night."

"Are you sure it's the one?"

"Sure I'm sure, I've seen her before, loads of time. David never stopped looking at the picture; he was so angry."

"About what?"

"She fingered him out of sheer spite. He served nine years for armed robbery because of that woman, and he wanted compensation."

"He didn't want to kill her?"

"David wasn't a killer, though maybe with her, he might have made an exception."

"Are you sure that she's got the money?"

"Positive."

"I don't see why you are so angry with her; you weren't even that close to Blake."

"I wasn't, but he was a friend and let me stay here when I didn't have anywhere else to go. I just want the money, that's all. I need it more than she does. Here's the address. You tell her that you are going to the police, and she will hand over the money."

"Either that or stick a knife in me."

"She's not going to do that. Tell her you are there to make her an offer on behalf of some other people. Tell her that you know she killed David and that she has the money. She will know that if anything happens to you, then she will get fingered for another murder.

"You're very confident when other people are taking the risks."

"You're getting well paid."

"Maybe I should be getting the biggest share. Shouldn't that be sixty forty to me?"

"Get out of here. I will expect you back in a couple of hours with a case of money."

The door opened suddenly and caught me off guard. Gittins saw me, but I don't think my face registered straight away. It did with Breanna.

"That's the bloke who came around snooping. Get him, Harry."

Harry must have remembered me as well because he let out a roar and charged. I sidestepped and hit him with a left hook as he went sailing past. He grabbed at my coat on his way to the floor, his nose caught on the buckle of my belt, and he grunted with pain before blacking out.

"He never was much of a fighter, was H." She stood over his head with her legs apart. I thought that she was going to grind one of her stiletto heels into his face, but she resisted the temptation and smiled at me seductively.

"I like a man who can defend himself. Did you hear that conversation back there?"

I nodded.

"I don't suppose I could tempt you?"

I shook my head, and she deflated in front of me, and then threw a quite acceptable right hook.

I caught her hand, patted her head playfully, and let it go.

"Now you're a Feisty one, Breanna. Can't get your own way and try to hit a guy who is only doing his job. I think we need to sit down and talk. Put the kettle on."

CHAPTER SIXTEEN

In the end, it was me that had to make the tea. Breanna sat upright on one of the wooden chairs and stared at me. She never answered when I asked if she wanted one or two spoonfuls of sugar.

While I was waiting for the water to boil in an old saucepan, I walked over to Harold. He was still not moving, and his eyes were closed. I went into his coat pocket and pulled out a piece of paper. I assumed it was the address that she had written for him. It was 12 Lightfoot Street. The address of the band. No surprise there.

I finished making the tea, took a cup over to Breanna, and handed it to her.

I sat down on the only other chair in the room. "All this excitement has given me a thirst. Do you want to tell me what this is all about?"

"Why should I? You're not the police. I don't need to tell you anything, but I will ask you something."

"What?"

"Do you want to make the easiest ten thousand pounds ever?"

"I thought that Harry was going to make forty thousand. Do I take it that you know where the money is and who murdered David Blake?"

"I do. I will give you thirty thousand if you help me. Come on. I thought that people bought your services. That is what I want to do. Get me the money, and I will split it. Who will know?"

"I will know, Breanna."

"Stop talking in riddles. OK, I will split it with you forty, sixty. I can't do any better than that."

"How about you and your pal come and pay a visit to the police. I think that you could be looking at theft and murder as a starter."

"I never killed anybody, and I don't have any money. Just because I know where it is, doesn't make me a thief."

"If you think anything about David Blake, you would want to bring his murderer to justice. Where is your morality, Breanna?"

"Okay. I can see what you are doing. We split it fifty, fifty, but that is my last offer."

I sighed and got up. Let's go."

"Go where?"

"To see the police. I'm tired of this; let them sort it out. I hope you have got a good alibi."

There was a sound near the door. We both looked over. It was Harry Gittins getting to his feet. He looked shaky but managed to open the door and looked ready to run.

"I don't think that you will be needing me, Mr Shannon. Let me go, and I will tell you everything that I know."

"You bastard," hissed Breanna. She made a move to get up, but I grabbed her arm. She tried to bite me, so I squeezed until she cried out in pain.

She settled back down on the chair and went back to her sulking.

"What do you know, Harry?"

"David Blake was grassed on and has been trying to find the woman who did it since he got out of prison. He has carried around a picture of her and showed it to just about everybody he met, including me. He was a real bore if he had a few drinks. He would go on and on about what he was going to do to her when he found her. I don't know the details, but apparently, he found her and winded up dead for his troubles. Breanna saw a documentary on some pop group that has just reformed. There were some old pictures of wives and girlfriends, and she recognised one of them from a picture David used to carry around with him."

"I want a name."

"And I want out of here, Mr Shannon. You get the name, and I go home. We both forget that this ever happened."

"OK."

"Her name is Christine Finn, and that's all you are going to get out of me." With that, he left, and I heard him fire up the Mercedes and drive off in a squeal of burning rubber and smoke.

CHAPTER SEVENTEEN

The house in Lightfoot Street looked abandoned. There was a little red mini in the drive but no signs of life inside as I strolled up to the main door. I rang the bell and waited. I wasn't optimistic and was rewarded for my paranoia with nothing.

I walked around the side of the house and passed a double garage that had the door open. It was empty. I went through a gate in the middle of a wooden fence and found myself in a large garden with a swimming pool enclosed in a very large structure that looked like a greenhouse. This must have been the pool where the body had been found.

I was confronted with the unusual sight of Hilary Crash pegging out washing on a clothesline. It was so out of character from what the wife of a rock star should have been doing that it brought a wry smile to my lips.

Her welcoming smile in return when she caught sight of me, I knew, was not going to last very long.

"Come over, Mr Shannon. Have you got any news about the money?"

"I have news on the money and the murder. How is that for earning my wages?"

She pegged a faded pair of blue jeans at the end of the clothesline and walked towards me. "Come in; we can discuss it over a drink. I hope that Fire is going to get his money back; he hasn't so much as smirked once since he came back from Scotland."

"I don't blame him. That's a lot of money we're talking about."

"Have you found it, Mr Shannon?"

"I have not physically got my hands on the money or the murderer, but I'm closing in, Christine."

"Sorry?"

"I said that I'm closing in, Christine." Did I see a slight hint of her face colouring, or was it my imagination?

She hesitated, and her body language went defensive. "Why are you calling me that name?"

"Because that is your name. Aren't you Christine Finn, or am I mistaken?"

She picked up her washing basket and threw in the unused pegs.

"You'd better come in. I can explain over coffee."

The smell of freshly cut flowers in the living room was pungent and overpowering. I wanted to ask if we could open the window or talk in the garden, but she insisted on making us coffee and left me on my own. She took so long that by the time she came back, I was worried that she had run out on me. When she appeared carrying a silver tray with a pot of coffee and biscuits on it, I concluded that she had just needed time to think about what she was going to say.

She sat down in a leather armchair and poured out the coffee. "Help yourself to biscuits, Mr Shannon. You must be tired and hungry after all of the digging you have been doing in the dirt."

That was a punch below the belt. "Just doing my job, Hilary, or do you prefer Christine?"

"Hilary will do just fine."

I drank some coffee and took a chocolate bourbon cream off the plate. She settled back in her chair and stared at me like I was something unpleasant that she had found under her shoe. "What do you want to know, Mr Shannon?"

"The truth would be nice?"

"I don't know where to start. Why don't you ask me a question?"

"Do you admit that you are Christine Finn?"

"I changed my name, but there are reasons."

"Such as?"

"Such as I was scared and also a little bit ashamed of my past."

"What were you scared of?"

"In Wakefield, I got in with the wrong crowd, and I met David when I was only fourteen."

"You're talking about David Blake?"

"Of course. Back in those days, he was dishy, and all of my mates fancied him. You could say that I was the lucky winner, but Dave turned out to be the booby prize."

"Why was that?"

"I was fourteen, and he was ten years older. He could have almost been my father but acted like an older brother. With David, you did what he said or else."

"Or else what?"

"Or else you would get a good hiding."

"So, you are saying that he hit you."

"That's a very gallant way of putting it, Mr Shannon. What he used to do was despicable, and I'm not going to go into it. Let's just say, if he thought that I had done something wrong; then at the very least, he would take his belt off and thrash me with it."

"What do you mean by doing something wrong?"

"Oh, you know, the usual things. If he thought that I was looking at another lad, he would hit me. If a lad was looking at me, he would hit me. If I didn't do what he said, he would hit me."

"I've met your mum, Christine…"

"Don't call me that. I'm Hilary now, and that's how I want to stay."

"As I said, I've met your mum. She doesn't seem to be the type of woman to let this happen."

"My mum was scared of David. Lots of people in Wakefield didn't like him, but nobody had the guts to stand up to him."

"Yes, but you could have told him you wanted out and finished with him."

"He would never have let that happen. It would have damaged his male ego. The only way I would have got out of that relationship is if he had got tired of me."

"And you are saying that this was never going to happen."

"No. He was getting more and more jealous. Also, he was always giving things to me to stash for him. We used to keep the stuff in the old vegetable cellar out in the shed. Whenever he did a job, he would turn up and stash the stuff there until he could get it fenced. He was part of a gang. David used to steal the stuff, and there was somebody else who would get rid of it."

"What sort of stuff are we talking about?"

"Anything, but mainly booze and cigarettes. They were easy to get rid of and easy to store. Funny, but I remember one time that the police called at our house with a warrant. It was for something completely different. They thought that my dad had robbed a meat warehouse. My mum was bricking it, but they never even found the trap door of the cellar."

"And had he?"

"Had he what?"

"Had your dad robbed a warehouse?"

"Of course, but the daft man tried to sell it down the pub and got caught. He tried to sell pork chops to an undercover cop. He got six months for that."

"I get the impression that you were a downtrodden, misunderstood victim that wanted to get out of her life. Am I right?"

"Now, you are laughing at me. It's OK for you. Look at the size of you. You must be six foot three?"

"Six, four."

How can you understand? Six feet four, with a face that would scare anybody. Who would ever pick on you?"

"You would be surprised, Hilary. But let's get back to the plot. What made you decide to do it?"

"To do what?"

"To get away from David Blake after how many years?"

"Seven."

"Was it the seven-year itch?"

"The what?"

Never mind. What made you want to grass him to the police?"

"I had come to the end. If I hadn't, then I think my mum would have done it. My dad had just died, and she had given up caring."

"Did you tell the cops about the warehouse robbery?"

"Those cops were a shower of evil bastards. I told them about the robbery, and they promised to put me somewhere out of harm's way. After they arrested him, they said that there was no need, so I disappeared. I changed my name and the rest, as they say, is history."

"History up to a point. You are forgetting that David Blake found you and winds up dead. Did you kill him, Hilary?

"You have got to be kidding. Do I look like a killer?"

"Killers come in all different shapes and sizes. There isn't an actual look that you need to have to be one. What about the money? Did you take that?"

"No. I didn't kill David, and I didn't take the money. All that happened was he came to see me."

"He came to see you, and you gave him a coffee and some bourbon creams, and he left? Yeah, that will go down well in court in front of a jury."

"Court? Jury? It's not going to get to that, is it?"

"Not if you are innocent, and you tell me the truth."

"The truth is that I am as much in the dark as you. He turned up and said that I owed him for the time he had spent in prison. He said that if it hadn't been for me, he would have been a rich man. He wanted compensation."

"What did you say?"

"I asked him what he wanted and true to form, he said money. He thought that Connor and I were rich. I told him that it was just Fire that had the money. He said that if that was the case, then I should get it off him."

"How much money did he ask for?"

"That's just it. He said that I should decide how much money would compensate for nine years in prison."

"You never asked him how much he wanted"

"No, I was in a panic that Connor would come back and find him in the house. I told him that I would see what I could do. He left, and I never saw him again."

"That doesn't sound very convincing."

"I am not that bothered about you being convinced. If you had been there, you would have understood. He had a way about him that made you afraid. He also said as he was leaving that if he didn't think that it was enough money, then he would take the rest out on me."

"And you never saw him after that?"

"On my life; no."

CHAPTER EIGHTEEN

It was irrelevant whether I believed Hilary Crash or not. My main concern was that I couldn't prove anything, and I was still no closer to getting the money back. I drove home and stopped by my office to check my mail and messages.

It was closing in on lunchtime when I unlocked the door, and the first thing that I noticed was the little red light of my answerphone flashing. It was a message from Forrest Moore at the police records department. He wanted me to ring him back.

It took a while getting through, but he eventually picked up just as I was about to put down the receiver and go for something to eat. Why did I get the impression that he had been sleeping? Maybe it was the drowsiness in his voice.

"Mr Shannon, I think that I have dug something up that you might be interested in. Do you want to come in and have a look?"

"Can you tell me over the phone?"

He seemed to find this amusing. "No, better in person."

As I walked back to my car, I had the feeling that Moore didn't get many visitors to his old records cellar. I wondered if this was going to be a useful trip or if he was just craving company.

On my way over, I made an impulse decision. I needed to pass by the Eastmoor Estate on my way to the Wakefield Police Records Department, and as I didn't expect Forrest Moore to have very much for me, maybe Elsie Finn could solve the mystery about the money.

It was raining heavily by the time I reached her council house. It was still neat enough, but the rain had given the whole area a very different vibe. Whereas the last time I had come, it had felt menacing, in the cold, grey drizzle, the street felt gloomy.

I walked up the garden and knocked on the front door. I was still knocking five minutes later, so I went around the back. I looked in through the kitchen window and confirmed in my head that she was out before going to the front of the house again. I hadn't noticed it on my first visit, but there was a small wooden shed in the corner of the garden. Could it be that old habits don't die?

I was still not convinced that Hilary Crash was not someway involved in the murder and the robbery. She had told me herself that they used to stash stuff in the cellar of the shed. Maybe she has stashed the money there? It was more than a long shot, but it was all that I had.

I made sure that there was nobody on the street and got out my housebreaking tool kit. This consisted of several pieces of wire on a key ring. The lock was a pushover, and I was in the shed in seconds. It was dark but not dark enough for me not to notice the threadbare rug, with an old tin bath lying on top of it.

I rolled the bath off it and pulled up the rug. The pull-up door of the cellar fitted almost perfectly into the floorboards. I grabbed at the metal ring at the side and eased it open. It came up as if it was still used regularly, and my optimism soared. I walked down the wooden steps and got out my pencil flashlight.

It was a small cellar and it smelt of apples. It wasn't very high, so I needed to stoop so low that in the end, I had to get on my knees. I shone the light around the room. It was glaringly empty. I wondered if I should check for a secret panel, but even I wasn't that optimistic.

I climbed out and put everything back in order. As I was doing so, a car pulled up on the street outside. I pushed the bath back on the rug and made my way out as quickly as I could.

There was a nondescript Ford parked behind my Riley Elf, and the occupants seemed very interested in the fact that I had just come out of the shed. I stayed where I was and waited for them to join me.

Elsie Finn was first out. She had been sitting in the back, behind Hilary Crash and Bruce Rush.

Now, this was going to make an interesting story, especially as they had not had time to make up any lies.

"Chance meeting with your daughter while shopping?" I asked.

She pushed past me and opened the door. "We can explain everything. I hope this is going to stay between you and us."

CHAPTER NINETEEN

Elsie Finn made a cup of tea, and I sat opposite Bruce Rush and Hilary Crash, waiting for her to finish. She eventually appeared and set the pot of tea and cups down on the table. She poured out the steaming liquid and sat down.

"Help yourself to milk and sugar. Now, I think that it is up to Christine to explain everything. After all, it was her that got us all into this mess."

Hilary put milk and sugar into the tea and placed the cup and saucer on her lap. "I haven't got that money, Mr Shannon, and I didn't kill David. You've got to believe me."

"I don't think it's a question of whether I believe you; it's going to be up to the police."

"Do we have to involve them?"

"I think that Fire will want to get them involved in some way if he doesn't get his money back. All I need is the truth. If you tell me the truth, who knows, I might be able to help you."

"What is truth, Mr Shannon?"

"Don't go all philosophical on me, Hilary. You know as well as I do what truth is."

"I told you the truth about David. He was a scary character. He would have never let me go. That's why I needed to disappear and get a new life."

"Yeah, but you didn't need to put him in prison."

"I think that I did. David would have found me and killed me."

"Not if you had just left. I think that he was angry about spending nine years in prison because of you."

"I had to do it."

"Why?"

She looked at her mum. "Go on, Christine, it's going to come out anyway."

"David was part of a gang that was well known around the town. They called themselves the Forty-Thieves. I got pretty close to another member of the gang. "

"What was his name?"

"His name was Liam. Liam Hass. Anyway, one thing led to another, and I found out that I was pregnant."

Elsie Finn sighed heavily. "Never could keep her legs closed, Mr Shannon."

"What would David Blake have done if he had found out?"

"Killed both of us. You can understand why I was scared?"

"Yeah, I'm beginning to get the picture."

"Anyway, it all happened at once. They did this big warehouse job the day before I found out that I was pregnant. I told the police about David, and I ran away to Lightfoot Street to stay with Connor."

"You're telling me that you were going out with David Blake, pregnant by Liam Hass, and living with Connor Crash."

"Yes."

"She's a tart, Mr Shannon," said Mrs Finn reaching for a packet of cigarettes.

"It wasn't like that," said Hilary. "I had been seeing Connor for six months. I met him when the band played in Wakefield. Connor was different. He said that he wanted to marry me. What else could I do?"

"What did you say to Hass?"

"That's just it. Hass turned out to be worse than David. He came to the house and threatened to tell Connor that we had been having an affair while I was going out with him."

"It was an accident before you ask," said Elsie Finn."

"What was an accident?" I asked anyway.

"When he came to see me in Lightfoot Street. He turned up at the end of a party and threatened to tell Connor everything. We had an argument, I pushed him, and he fell over a beer crate and hit his head on the side of the pool."

"That's who the body was that they discovered?"

She nodded. "But it was an accident."

"Wasn't he found floating in the pool with no clothes on? Are you saying that he turned up to the party nude?"

"No. I realised he was dead. I stripped him and pushed him in the water. What else could I do?"

"Call an ambulance?"

"He was dead," said Elsie Finn

"You can't prove any of this anyway. What harm has it done?"

"I think that it did enough harm to Liam Hass."

"He was a pig. If Connor had found out that I was pregnant, he would have finished with me. He was almost as jealous as David, though in a more gentle way."

"You could have told him that it was his baby."

"Impossible."

"Why?"

"Connor can't have children; he told me when we started going out. He was very sensitive about it."

"Wasn't Fire accused of killing Hass?"

"It wasn't my fault that he came to the pool room, wrecked out of his head, and fell asleep. Nobody used the swimming pool. That's why I took Liam in there to talk. I thought that it would make things simpler. A body in the pool? It's your typical rock star incident. How was I to know that it was going to split the band up?"

"Do you expect me to believe all of this?"

"Yes. It's the truth."

"But you didn't murder David Blake, and you don't have the money."

"No."

"Hang on a minute. You said that you were pregnant and you couldn't tell Connor. Did you get rid of the baby?"

"Why do you think I spent more than nine months away from everybody? I told Connor that I was going into rehab. He believed me, and even gave me the money, but I was really back here going through a very difficult pregnancy. Connor and the boys were too busy trying to get their careers back on track in Germany. Connor probably didn't even know that I was gone. That's the thing about being married to a rock star. Fame is a difficult mistress to have to compete with."

"You had the baby here?"

"Yes. Natural birth."

"What happened to it? Did somebody adopt it?"

"That would be me," said Elsie Finn.

"So, where is the baby?"

"That baby grew up to be me," said Bruce Rush. "Confusing, isn't it?"

CHAPTER TWENTY

I knew that rock music and the people that made it were crazy, but Beasley Street had to be the weirdest of them all. Bruce Rush had been brought up by Elsie Finn as her son, when in fact, he was the son of her daughter.

It was his idea to get the band back together, so he changed his name and persuaded all of the members of Beasley Street that they could make a comeback and generate lots of money. I couldn't take many more revelations, so I made my excuses and left. They were a bunch of liars, but I was no nearer solving the death of David Blake, or who had got the money.

On the positive side, I now knew who the body was in the swimming pool, and I knew that Hilary Crash was capable of murder. From what I knew about her, she was capable of anything, but there was also no way I could prove it. Even her mother said she was a tart, and had added as I left the house. "She is a carbon copy of her father; god rest his soul."

I made my way to the police records department, and by the time I arrived, I had decided to give up the case and move on. I hated rock music, and I hated rock musicians and their entourage; but above all, I hated Beasley Street.

Forrest Moore was in his cubicle looking for winners in the racing pages of the Daily Mirror Newspaper. He looked like he wanted to be somewhere else, and I couldn't blame him because I did too.

"Feeling lucky, Forrest?"

"I'm doing a double at Kempton Park this afternoon, Morris. I've got a friend who is a stable lad on the Wirral. He's given me two certainties. Good price as well."

"You said that you had something for me?"

"Yes. I was thinking after you left, and I did a bit of digging. That lad you were talking about."

"David Blake?"

"That's the one. I didn't know anything about him personally, but did you know that he was a member of a very famous gang in Wakefield?"

"The Forty-Thieves?"

His face dropped. "Oh, you do know. I thought that it was my little secret. I was looking through their file. Nothing big, but they robbed a fair bit of stuff in their day. Never caught, but David Blake confessed to lots of unsolved cases when they brought him in. That was very convenient for us because it made our crime detection rate a lot better."

"Is that it?"

"Yes. I thought that it might help you, but as you already know."

I felt even more deflated now. "It's a stupid name for a gang."

"I agree, Morris, especially as there were only three members. One of them disappeared."

"Yeah, that was Liam Hass."

Now it was his turn to look deflated. "You certainly have been doing some serious detecting work, Morris. Blake grassed on Hass, but we never got him. He disappeared. The file is still open. I don't know how it ended up down here."

I wondered if I should tell him but decided against it. The whole thing was too complicated. "What do you think happened to Hass?"

"Haven't a clue, Morris. He didn't have a family, just a string of girlfriends. He was a bit of a lad was Liam. Nasty piece of work."

"You said that there were three members. Was the other one caught?"

"Not a chance. I think he was the mastermind. He was the person that got rid of the stuff, but they never did find him."

I thanked him for his trouble, and he handed me a grey folder stuffed with paper.

"I don't know if you want this, but I did a photocopy of all of the material on the Forty-Thieves. If you don't take it, I will throw it away."

I took it off him, thanked him again, and headed for my car.

CHAPTER TWENTY-ONE

It was late afternoon when I arrived at Shoddy's flat. He was watching TV and drinking Polish Cherry Vodka from a shot glass. I filled him in on my visit, and he didn't say anything until I'd finished. He went over to the fridge and brought out a pack of streaky bacon.

"Fancy a sandwich? We could nip down the pub later and have a session on the money that we've earned."

"What about the case?"

"What about it? It looks like we have come to the end. The ransom money has gone, and whoever has it is probably on a beach somewhere in the Caribbean, laughing their head off. You can't solve the murder of David Blake, and nobody is interested anyway."

"What about the body in the swimming pool? I know who did that."

"And what good is it going to do you telling the cops about Hilary Crash, or should I say, Christine Finn? You don't have any proof, it happened years ago, and from what you said about Liam Hass, he was a bit of a nasty lad that was trying his luck to blackmail a pregnant woman."

"Let's leave it. Shall I telephone?"

"Do it in the morning. You never know, they might want to keep you on as security."

"I doubt it, and besides, I'm not a bodyguard; I'm a detective."

Shoddy snorted and brought out some eggs. "Toast or bread?"

"Toast."

I watched the TV as Shoddy cooked. There was nothing very interesting on, and I flicked through the channels and turned it off. I picked up the file that Forrest Moore had given me and opened it. There were a couple of police reports on robberies. They all ended with a red stamp that said solved, with a numbered reference. The references must have been other files, but Forrest hadn't included them. The final page in the file was written by a police inspector, and it was headed, The Forty-Thieves.

I skipped through the first page, which was a list of robberies that had occurred in Wakefield in the late 1960s. They were all marked either committed or suspected committed by the Forty-Thieves.

The name had been around for a few years in Wakefield, but it was only after the arrest of David Blake that anything was known about the gang.

David Blake had a reputation as a violent compulsive thief who had a history of juvenile crimes that included grievous bodily harm and attempted murder. He was a lot heavier a character than I had first thought. It looked like he had spent most of his teenage years inside various juvenile correction institutions. There was a psychiatric report on him that concluded he was unstable.

I understood why Christine Finn had changed her name and ran away after grassing him to the police, but it looked like David Blake had done his own grassing. He had told the police about Liam Hass and admitted that he had done a long list of robberies in an attempt to get a lesser sentence. It seemed to have worked because he came out in nine years.

The file ended with a hospital report on the injured guard and a final note about the third member of the gang. It seemed that even though David Blake was prepared to throw his partner, Liam Hass, to the wolves, he was not prepared to do the same for the third member. Loyalty? The police report thought that it was more a question of him being scared than anything honourable.

David Blake said that he had never met or spoken to the third gang member, whose job it was to get rid of the goods that had been stolen. Blake claimed that all of the dealings were through a third party and that the third party was never the same person twice. All that he could say about the third member of the gang was that it was him that had thought up the name Forty-thieves and that everybody called him Gonzo.

There was a call to all cops to find out who Gonzo was. As the file ended there, it looked like they never succeeded.

Gonzo... Speedy Gonzales. As Shoddy passed me a mug of tea, I shot out of my chair, reached for my car keys, and headed for my car.

Albert Cross, known to his mates as Gonzo, was Breanna

Holcomb's ex-landlord and had a lot of explaining to do. I only

hoped that I wasn't too late.

CHAPTER TWENTY-TWO

If Albert Cross was surprised to see me when he opened the door, he didn't show it.

"You'd better come in, Mr Shannon," was his initial reaction. I was more surprised that he had remembered my name.

On the journey to his house, I had rehearsed what I was going to say to him. I was going to start with "Hello, Gonzo," in the hope that it would wipe any smile off his face as he realised that the game was up. As it panned out, it was me who had been knocked off balance by his cool response, and I followed him like a lamb into the same room that I had talked to him on my previous visit.

This time, there were two half-full glasses of what looked like whisky on the coffee table. He handed me one of them and simpered.

"I saw you pull up in your car. I assumed that you were coming to see me, as I am the only house for at least a quarter of a mile."

I took a sip. It was good quality single malt. "I suppose that you know why I am here."

"I can guess. I'm surprised that it took you so long. It was a bit of a slip of the tongue, me telling you my nickname was Gonzo. To be fair, though, I didn't think that you would be that clever to work it out."

Was that a compliment or an insult? He sat down, and I sat down opposite.

"You also made a mistake giving me the name of the shop where Breanna Holcomb is staying."

"Yes, I realise now, but at the time, I thought that the shop was empty. David never told me that he had taken her in. I didn't think they were that close. She is scum, of course, but that is the sort of woman that David used to like. No brains and no morals. You know the kind, Mr Shannon."

"Before I call the police, do you want to tell me what this is all about?"

"Willingly, Mr Shannon. Now, where shall I start? He didn't wait for me to reply. "You know that David had been in prison for quite of few years. To say that when he came out, he was a bitter man is an understatement."

"Bitter because of being grassed by his girlfriend?"

"Of course."

"But how did he find out?"

"She told Liam Hass, and when she disappeared, he told David. Then, of course, Liam disappeared. I assumed that they had run off together."

"No. She murdered him."

"Now, I didn't know that, but it doesn't surprise me. Girls like Christine Finn are unique. She was dangerous, and of course, a real slag. Her family was the same. The Finn family had a reputation in Wakefield."

"Shall we get to the point of my visit, Mr Cross?"

"Please, call me Gonzo."

"Okay, get to the point, Gonzo."

"I kept in touch with David while he was in prison and let him have the cottage when he came out. He didn't stay very long. I suppose he found the place a bit too isolated. I noticed how bitter he had become for those lost years in prison. He wanted to find Christine and make her pay."

"How did he find her?"

"There you go again, Mr Shannon, rushing me through my story. First things first; do you want a top-up?"

I offered him my glass, and he filled it almost to the brim with whisky."

"I do believe that you are trying to get me drunk, Gonzo. It will take more than a couple of glasses."

He ignored me and lit a cigar. It was a big golden brown Havana. I hate the smell of those. "David turned up later with Breanna. I didn't like the look of her, but he persuaded me to let her stay in the cottage. It's true about the reference letter. The company that leases the place out insist."

"How did Blake manage to get his hands on a second-hand shop?"

"He didn't. It's mine. He stayed there for a couple of weeks. When I gave you that address, it was to get rid of you. I knew that David wasn't there, but I didn't know that he had given Breanna a key. I assumed that the shop was empty."

"Is this the shop that you used to sell the stuff that Liam Hass and David Blake stole?"

"It is, or rather was. I've retired. The shop is up for sale. Do you fancy buying it?"

"Did you kill David Blake?"

"We were a great team, the three of us. It was me that thought up the name the Forty- Thieves. A gang needs a name, don't you think, Mr Shannon?"

"Did you kill David Blake?"

"David Blake deserved what was coming. He will not be missed."

"That may be the case, but how did he find Christine Finn?"

"That would be me."

I turned around and there standing by the door, was Bruce Rush. He came over and sat on the edge of Gonzo's chair. "He didn't find mum; I told him where she was."

"That wasn't very nice of you, Mr Rush. Was it you that killed him?"

He looked at Gonzo, and I noticed that Gonzo slightly nodded his head.

"I told Blake where to find mum, and then told him that the best way to get money was to get Fire's wife to pay a ransom. I persuaded the boys to disappear to Fire's country retreat in Scotland, wrote the note, and waited for the money to arrive. As soon as Blake had the money, Gonzo killed the bastard."

"I did, Mr Shannon, and I can honestly say that I rather enjoyed it."

"But how did you all know each other?"

Gonzo smirked and poured some more whisky into my glass. "Why do you think that Christine's mum felt safe enough to bring up Bruce in Wakefield?" He didn't want an answer. "She was safe because I protected them. Me and Christine's mum go back a long way. She should have married me, not that loser of a husband she ended up with. But that's water under the bridge now. This money is for the Finns to start a new life. Christine will be OK with that rock star of a husband. I don't want any of it. I have enough all ready to retire."

I was about to say something, but for a couple of minutes, my head had been playing tricks, and it was as if Gonzo and Bruce Rush's voices were coming from inside a cave. They were getting further and further away. I tried to stand up, but my head started to spin. I could hear Gonzo laughing but now couldn't see them. The last thing I heard was the front door slamming and the sound of a powerful engine starting up and then disappearing into the distance.

EPILOGUE

"Turn that noise down, Shod. What is it you are watching, anyway?"

I had just come back from the office and was surprised to see my partner watching a pop band on TV.

"It's Top of the Pops, Moggsy. Don't you recognise the band?"

I looked at the screen and saw Fire. His blond hair reached his shoulders and must have been a wig. The rest of the band, Including Connor Crash, didn't get much camera attention, and the song that they were playing was one I had heard them do in the studio. It didn't sound any better on the TV.

"Is dinner ready?" I asked

Shoddy got up, switched channels, and went over to the oven. "I've made us a Shepherd's Pie, but it's going to be at least another ten minutes."

I didn't mind; I wasn't very hungry anyway. I got a beer from the fridge and settled down in front of the TV. I suppose that I was lucky just to be able to see the screen. Gonzo had put a powerful sleeping tablet in the whisky, but it could have been something more permanent than a four-hour sleep.

When I woke up, I went straight round to see Hilary Crash, and she must have known about what had happened because she was a lot less cagy than before. She also gave me a couple of hundred pounds for my trouble and told me that my services would no longer be needed.

In return, I had told her about being drugged and the disappearance of Gonzo with her son.

She transfixed me with an intense stare. "Can I level with you, Mr Shannon?"

"I don't know, can you?"

"I will never say this in a court of law, but I think that you deserve an explanation for the way you have been treated."

I agreed with her that I did.

"When Liam Hass came around and threatened me, I was telling you the truth about him falling back and hitting his head.

"But?"

"But, I never told you what I did after."

"I'm all ears. What did you do?"

"I telephoned Gonzo. Of course, I already knew about his relationship with my mum, and I also knew that he was somebody that you didn't mess with."

"What did he do?"

"He came to the house, told me to make myself scarce, and that he would sort it. And that is what he did."

"You are telling me that Gonzo murdered Liam Hass and David Blake?"

"Yes. You can never prove it, and even if you did, Gonzo, my mum, and Bruce are in a country where you could never touch them."

Was she telling me the truth? I couldn't say for sure, but my gut feeling was that she was.

And that was that. She continued her life with Beasley Street and Gonzo, Elsie Finn and Bruce Rush were probably enjoying the good life on Fire's hundred thousand. They were probably in Spain, as there was no extradition agreement for criminals between Spain and Britain. What did I care?

To be honest, I didn't. I was just glad it was all over.

Shoddy filled me in later that, in his opinion, they had probably gone somewhere more exotic to live, as Spain signed an extradition agreement in 1985. I don't know why, but I could see the three of them in some South American backwater.

You don't have to like your clients to be able to work for them, but I think that I hated pop music even more than I did before. In future, I am going to stick to cases that have nothing to do with music unless, of course, it is German Marching Band music.

The only thing about the case that puzzles me still is why Christine Finn's son changed his name to Bruce Rush. Was his name Bruce Finn? If not, what was his real name?

Shoddy analysed the reason why in his usual clear and logical way. When it came to Beasley Street, they had all changed their names. Why?

Because that's the music business.

Roll on the next case.

The End

Thank you for reading the Penny Detective.

If you enjoyed it, pass it on and tell some of your friends.

Visit my author page here: <u>Visit Amazon's John Tallon Jones</u>
<u>Page</u> (This is my mailing list)

If you want to contact me with any comments, ideas, or thoughts about the book, or just for a chat, look me up on:

Facebook: https://www.facebook.com/john.t.jones.52

Email me at john151253@gmail.com

I always reply and am always very happy to hear from you.

Books in the Penny Detective Series are:

The Penny Detective

The Italian Affair

An Evening with Max Climax

The Shoestring Effect

Chinese Whispers

Murder at Bewley Manor

Dead Man Walking

The Hangman Mystery

Flawed

The Black Rose Murders

The Elephant Room

A Simple Case of Murder

Murder at Woodley Grange

The Contender

The Mentalist

A Death in the Family

Murder at the Voodoo Lounge

Candy's Room

The Trouble with Nigel

The Murder Club

Beasley Street

Other Books by John Tallon Jones

Inspector Visco:

The Lady from Rome

The Sicilian Assassin

Cheer

Solid Air

Andy Marsh Investigates:

A Lesson in Terror

Dangerous People

Dark Harvest

The Deadly Sleeper

Before you go, here are a couple of chapters from another book in the series called

Murder at the Voodoo Lounge

CHAPTER ONE

I didn't realise that vegetables could be so heavy, but I put it down to my twenty-minute run as I tried to catch the person who had stolen them. I was definitely out of condition, but my big overcoat and Wellington boots hadn't helped. The coat was for the chilly night air and the Wellingtons for the mud. I still wasn't too sure if it had been a man or a woman I had been chasing because they were well covered up. In the end, they had thrown the bags at the side of the canal, and I had stopped to pick up the contents. This consisted mainly of potatoes, carrots, turnips, cabbages, and cauliflowers.

It was early morning but already hot. I had spent the best part of the night hiding behind bushes near an allotment in an attempt to catch the serial vegetable thief who had been terrorising the local gardeners. They had all banded together to pay my fee, and this had been my fourth night. I have to say that two of the previous three prolonged surveillance operations had ended with me fast asleep and that on this occasion, I had only woken up by chance. This was just in time to see the thief disappearing down the canal bank with two supermarket bags that were bulging.

Walking by the decaying canal on this deep summer morning made me wonder whatever happened to the idea of flowing, pristine clear water. From polystyrene fast-food packaging to the occasional bike and rusty pram, the Croxley canal was a place where no life existed, and weird-looking weeds grew to tropical proportions out of the dank, foul-smelling mud.

I was walking as fast as I could to get clear and was contemplating adding to the canal chaos by throwing in some of the potatoes when the sun peeped through from behind the disused gas works. It was reddish and was soon tangled up and hidden by fluffy white clouds that drifted in without the threat of rain. Maybe it was my imagination, or perhaps I was growing old, but even clouds were not the same these days. The ones above my head were tinged rusty-red as if they had been impregnated by chemicals, or some mad Salvador Dali type painter had turned them into one giant surrealist image. I searched for a hidden message in the sky but soon gave up and loosened my tie in deference to the rising temperature.

I needed a drink, but my watch showed that I had hours to wait until the pubs were once again open. I shuffled around a corner and passed under a bridge that led me into Greasby Street, which was a miasma of urbanised decay before I was even born and now had reached a pinnacle of epic dereliction.

Sitting on a white kitchen stool outside number thirty was a middle-aged lady wearing an orange Kaftan, with dyed red hair that emphasized the grey roots, and a heavily made-up face. She had applied blue eyeshadow to her eyelids and electric pink lipstick, which made her lips look well out of proportion to the rest of her face. Her eyebrows were penciled in and made her look permanently startled, like a rabbit caught in the headlamps of a car.

"Moggsy," she hooted as I tried unsuccessfully to make myself invisible. "Do you fancy a bit of fun before breakfast?"

"Depends on what type of fun, Doris."

Her face fell for just a fraction of a second, and then she got off her stool. "In your case, Moggsy, I'll put the kettle on, and we can have a nice cup of tea."

Doris was the local hooker and was an institution in this part of Croxley. She had been soliciting from her house ever since I was a child. No one knew how old she was or dared to ask, and the police turned a blind eye in exchange for information on low-life crime from time to time.

I followed her into a neat little room and sat down on a sofa while she poured hot water from a massive black kettle into a china blue teapot. She sat down with her legs apart as she waited for the tea to brew. The fact that she wasn't wearing underwear made me focus intently on her face, and she frowned as if she was wondering why. She seemed interested in my bags.

"Are those vegetables?"

"As far as I can make out," I said. I filled her in with the reason I was carrying them and gave her a Savoy cabbage.

"So, you are still dealing with major crime, Moggsy. Your dad must be turning in his grave."

"He's not dead, Doris. He's moved to Spain with mum."

"Well, turning over in his deckchair in Spain. You could have followed him into the used car business."

I changed the subject, not wanting to linger on the reasons why I had become a private detective. "Talking about business, Doris, how is yours?"

She handed me my tea in a cracked white porcelain mug. It was a thick as treacle and heavily sugared.

"Business comes and goes, but there is many a good tune played on an old fiddle. I've been at it so long I've had three generations of

Croxley families, though I never go with women." She lit a cigarette and drained her tea. "You have to draw the line somewhere, Morris."

I nodded my head sagely in illogical agreement and wondered if my dad had ever participated in Doris. I shuddered at the thought.

"Of course, I still have me regulars. They pay me quarterly, and I'm glad of that; some of the young lads come to me as well. I never charge any of them if it's their first time. They seem to like the idea of being started off by somebody with experience. Say what you want, I'm clean, and I always change the sheets every other day. Never had any diseases, and even after my husband died, have never been beaten up by a punter."

"Yeah, I heard about Jim dying. You must miss him."

"He was a useless piece of dog dirt; pardon my French. He never did a day's work in his life and sent me out to work on me back while he went to the pub. Still, I loved him, and he was faithful and was never jealous. Can you spare a couple of potatoes and carrots, Morris? I fancy a stew later."

I handed her some more vegetables and made a move towards the door.

"If you are ever lonely and fancy a bit of fun, you know where I am," she called after me as I went through the door. "There's many a good tune...."

"Played on an old fiddle. Yeah, I get your drift." I shouted back.

"Don't forget to tell your friends. I do discounts for parties, and two for the price of one."

Instantly, my best friend and business partner, Shoddy, sprang to mind. Maybe I would drop a word in his ear. Half an hour with Doris might do him a power of good.

I live in Croxley, which most people agree is at the arse-end of the world. It's just a collection of derelict buildings, with a sprinkling of pubs, shops, and offices. On any given day of the week, you can see gangs of jobless teenagers waiting to sell you drugs, or if they get desperate, beat you up and steal your wallet. Nothing good ever came out of Croxley, except the road to somewhere better. Working as a private detective here should have been lucrative because of the crime levels, but times were hard, and most of the crime was left unsolved because of this. Like always, I was thinking of ditching the job and finding something better. I had already gone for two interviews earlier on in the week with double glazing companies, but even they had turned me down.

Having given the vegetables back to their owner, I made my way home. This was a second floor flat in a high-rise complex that had been condemned as unfit for human habitation two decades ago. I ignored the lift, which seldom worked, and climbed the vomit and syringe littered stairs. I was breathing heavily and wheezing before I arrived at the door of my business partner Shoddy, who lived in an identical flat, which was next door to mine.

To somebody who was a total stranger, Shoddy would have thrown out a first-impression that screamed vagrant. As I went into his place and flung myself down on the sofa, he was stretched out in his favourite armchair with a can of cider in his hand and a cigarette dangling from his mouth. He reached over to the table and threw me a can, which I gratefully accepted. I opened it and winced at the taste.

"How did the stakeout go?" He asked. He turned the TV on in the same instance as if he already knew what my reply would be. He tuned in to the Open University Channel. There was a program on about how they had built the Panama Canal.

I put my hands into my coat pockets and pulled out some potatoes and carrots. I held up a turnip, like a trophy.

"Did they pay us in food, again?"

"No, they promised to give us some more money, but I declined the offer. Four nights behind a hedge is enough. Especially for the pittance, they were paying."

"A job is a job, Moggsy."

"That's right, so I told them that you might be interested."

He put both hands on his lower back and groaned. "You know me; I would be willing, but with my back, I wouldn't last an hour. I also would never be able to chase anybody with my feet problem."

"We had better hope a client phones up and wants to pay us in real money."

He lit another cigarette with the stub of the one he had just taken from his mouth. " What's the situation with new clients?"

"Woeful."

"Should we advertise?"

"Yeah, if you've got any money?"

"What about door to door?"

"What? Go around, knocking on doors to see if anybody needs a detective?"

"You never know, mate, it could work.

"I've sat for four days in the office waiting for somebody to call. I tell you, Shod, it's more depressing than hiding behind a hedge waiting for a burglar to start digging up vegetables."

"So nothing at all?"

"Just one order from somebody who thought he was phoning a Chinese takeaway and a lady who wanted her hair permed."

"You should have mentioned that you were a private detective."

"Yeah, you're right, Shoddy. I could have said that I didn't do egg fried rice, but if they knew of somebody who had died mysteriously, then I was their man."

"Don't get offended; it was just a suggestion."

After eating a vegetable stew for dinner and listening to even more stupid suggestions for getting clients, I stumbled into bed at midnight. I was seriously worried about the future and how I was going to make ends meet without a regular income. Outside was the usual collection of noises that glued the ambience of the area together. Dogs barking, delinquents joyriding on motorbikes up and down the streets, and police sirens wailing. Nothing out of the ordinary, but the sound of my telephone ringing was. It was so out of the ordinary that I actually ignored it for a good thirty seconds, and by the time I had sprung out of bed and dashed into my living room, I had almost given up that it would continue to ring. I put it tentatively to my ear.

"Hello."

"Is that Morris Shannon?"

"Speaking."

"And you are a private detective?"

"I am."

"I'm sorry to be ringing you at this late hour, but I was getting worried because you hadn't got back to me."

"Why should I be getting back to you?"

"You didn't read my note? You didn't answer your phone today, and your office was locked up, so I pushed it under your door."

"I have been busy with an important case," I lied. "Do you want to tell me what it is about?"

"Not really, Mr Shannon. Will you be in your office tomorrow?"

"Yes, most certainly."

"Then, all will be revealed. Goodnight:"

"Yes, but before you go..."

The phone went dead, and now I was sure that I wouldn't get any sleep. I pulled my emergency bottle of whisky out from the cupboard, wiped a dusty glass, and made my way onto my balcony. It was going to be a long night.

I was asleep within five minutes, dreaming of a big murder investigation in New York that took me to Hollywood and beyond.

CHAPTER TWO

On the floor of the office, when I arrived the next morning, was a piece of folded paper with a telephone number written on it. I looked at my watch; it was just after nine. I wondered if it was too early to telephone and came to the conclusion that it wasn't. There was no name written down on the paper, which could make it awkward. I dialled and decided to play it by ear.

"Hello?"

Was this the same voice that I had heard in my flat? "Hello, this is Morris Shannon. Was it you that telephoned me last night?"

"Ah, Mr Shannon, at last. Yes, it was me, and I would like to meet with you as soon as possible. When are you available?"

I pretended to turn pages in my diary by shuffling papers around my desk. When I was satisfied I hadn't exaggerated the action, I told him I was available right away because somebody had cancelled an appointment. He sounded relieved and also more than a bit drunk. I checked my watch again; it was five past nine.

"I'm staying at the Chichester Hotel in Aintree. Do you know it?"

"Yes, I think I have a vague idea where to find it."

"Shall we say two o'clock?"

"That's perfect. Who shall I ask for?"

"My name is Hershey, Jason Hershey."

"Like the American chocolate bar."

"Er... Yes, I suppose it is, though I'm not American. I'm from Brighton."

"Okay, Mr Hershey, I look forward to seeing you later."

The line went dead, and I went to the pub.

Shoddy was sitting in his usual chair in our local pub, which is strangely named The Old One Hundred. Nobody had ever worked out who the one hundred were and why they were old. Some ancient pictures of soldiers on the wall led most of the regulars to believe that the name was something to do with the First World War, but that was where the interest stopped.

"So, did you make contact with our new client?" He put down his newspaper, picked up his beer, and took a swig.

His name is Jason Hershey, and he's staying at the Chichester in Aintree."

"Like the American chocolate bar."

"Yeah, but I don't think he appreciated being told that."

"The Chichester is a five-star hotel, so he must have a bit of money. Let's hope it's something big."

"With our luck, he's probably lost his cat."

"Or his hamster," laughed Shoddy. "Are you are off to see him, or is he coming to see you?"

"I'm off to meet him."

Shoddy picked up his newspaper and turned to the racing results. "If you are going there, then make sure you get at least a couple of drinks out of him. Did you arrange to meet him in the bar?"

"No."

Shoddy shook his head. "You never learn. Let's hope you don't get stuck up in his bedroom."

"We could call room service."

Shoddy picked up the TV remote and flicked through the channels. I finished my drink and headed for the car park.

The Chichester was situated in a very select area of Aintree. In front of the tall, gleaming white building lay well-maintained gardens with steps leading up to an elegant lobby. The grounds were surrounded by a high redbrick wall that was topped with barbed wire and masked by mature pines.

I stopped at the front gate and rang the bell. A man wearing an elaborate grey uniform and a peaked cap came out of a small gatehouse. He had a boxer's cauliflower nose and skin that was wrinkled and saggy like an old Indian chief.

"We're full," he bellowed.

"I'm not deaf," I countered. "I'm here to meet somebody." This seemed to confuse him, and I wondered if he was going to let me in.

"Sorry." He ambled over to the gate, pressed a button, and opened it. "Who do you want to see?" he added a "Sir" at the end of his sentence but didn't seem convinced.

"I have an appointment with a Mr Hershey. He didn't say what it was about. My name is Morris Shannon."

A frown erupted slowly on his face. It started on his forehead and worked its way down. He beckoned me through. A middle-aged man in a white t-shirt and jeans came rushing around the corner and lunged at the entrance. His hat flew off, revealing a grey semi-bald head. Before he had a chance to make it into the garden, the doorman moved quickly and blocked his path. The man tried to dodge around him. The doorman punched him once to the stomach, and he went down on the pavement, groaning. He lay on the floor, shouting obscenities, and reached for his hat.

The doorman closed the gate quickly and locked it. His eyes were jaundiced like a snake, and his knuckles were bright red, where his fist had made contact with the other man's stomach.

The middle-aged man got up, painfully, to his feet. He stuck his head through the bars of the gate. His face had a profile that looked like it had been cut from sandstone; he had glaring bloodshot eyes and a thin mouth with spittle coming out of the sides.

"I'm going to get in to see Hershey if it takes me all day."

"Not on my watch, you won't," said the doorman.

"Then tell Hershey I want to see him."

"We've been through that before, mate, and I had to throw you out. If a client of this hotel doesn't want to see you, then you don't get to see him. When he is not a client anymore, then it's up to you and him to work it out. I haven't called the police so far, but I'm losing patience. Calm down and go home."

The man stood still behind the gate for a while, then seemed to change his mood.

"I'm sorry. I don't have any quarrel with you."

"That's not likewise, mate. I don't like you; now piss-off before I lose my temper. This is a five-star hotel, not the Salvation Army shelter for vagrants."

The middle-aged man turned his attention to me. Running his hand over his stomach as if to emphasise that it was hurting him. He sneered and spat through the gate, at the floor in front of where I was standing. "Are you one of Hershey's monkeys? He's as corrupt as they come. I feel sorry for anybody that works for him."

"I've never met the guy."

" Then why are you here to meet him? I heard you mention his name."

The doorman interrupted. "Are you going, or do I need to call the police?"

The man glared at me. "I'll go, only he had better be careful when he comes out, and he can't stay in your hotel forever."

I was curious now. "What's your problem with the man?"

"That's between him and me." He looked at me long and hard and spat again. "If you are going to see him, tell him that I have something very important to discuss with him."

"I suppose that I can tell him that, but who do I say the message is from?"

"Rufus Dixon, and it's about my daughter. You can also say that I won't be going anywhere until he agrees to meet me."

"Yeah, that's according to you, friend," the doorman said. "Now, bugger off, and I don't want to see you here again."

Rufus Dixon walked back up the street, moving at a snail's pace as if to show defiance. He dragged himself around the corner he had appeared from, and the doorman visibly relaxed and managed a grin. He licked his knuckles as if he had enjoyed the experience of violent behaviour.

"That bloke needs to see a doctor."

"Did you have to throw him out of the hotel?"

"Yeah. He turned up as I started my shift and said that he had an appointment with Mr Hershey."

"What made you throw him out?"

"This was at half-past six in the morning. I told him that we couldn't wake guests up that early and that he would have to come back at a more reasonable hour. When I told him this, he went ballistic and tried to run up the stairs. I grabbed him, put him in an arm lock, and threw him out." He smiled to himself as if he was remembering a fond memory. "I think I must have hurt him when I threw him onto the pavement. Still, he was lucky that I didn't phone the police. We try to deal with our problems without resorting to that at the Chichester."

"Very commendable."

I made my way into the lobby, which was painted in pastel colours and was tastefully furnished in a minimalistic fantasy of tainted glass and varnished wood. I wondered how much it cost a night to stay in a place like this, and what sort of a man I was about to meet. Through one of the glass doors, I could see an indoor swimming pool with an old man doing breaststroke lengths with an ease that made me jealous. Insipid music floated on the ice-cold air-conditioned atmosphere, and a young girl in a brilliantly white blouse, sitting behind a desk, smiled just a little bit too much as I approached. Her intelligent green eyes appraised me and came to the conclusion that I was not rich and was here to see somebody who was.

As if to confirm this, she said, "Mr Hershey is expecting you." She pointed to a glass lift and handed me a card which had room 312 written on it, to make sure I didn't forget. To confirm that I could read, she repeated the number twice and asked if I needed assistance to find the room. I assured her that I didn't, and she looked disappointed.

Three minutes later, after passing through a colour coordinated and sanitized corridor, I was knocking on the door.

"Who is it?" The voice sounded nervous and also slightly slurred. I suspected that he was still drunk.

"It's Morris Shannon. We have an appointment."

I heard at least two locks being clicked, and the door was opened ever so slightly. A fat face appeared in the ensuing crack; its eyes were washed out and pale, and its mouth was thin, and the lips cherry red and bulbous. The smell of alcohol that was released into the corridor confirmed at least one of my theories about my potentially new client.

"I'm glad you're here, Mr Shannon; it's not a moment too soon. You had better come in."

He made a big show of relocking the door behind me, and then he indicated for me to sit down on an elegant but very uncomfortable settee. Everything about this man was exaggerated, from his huge chubby bear-like frame to his gestures, which oozed tension and badly shot nerves.

He sat down opposite me and poured us both a drink, with hands that had a slight shake. He filled his glass to the top, while mine was barely wet at the bottom. It was fine old Tennessee sipping bourbon. I declined his offer of ice and lemonade, and he finished his and poured himself another. He was wearing a garish, red and yellow tartan shirt and lime green Chinos, which somehow didn't look strange on him despite his grey hair, boozers nose, and middle-aged face. He had one of those profiles that you couldn't tie down to an exact age. I went for mid-fifties but was prepared to be proved wrong.

I looked around his bedroom. It was large and as minimal as the rest of the hotel, though, for some reason only known to the designer, the walls were hung with pictures of erupting volcanoes. I wondered if there was some deep hidden meaning that the likes of somebody such as me could never understand.

Hershey applied a Zippo to a thick cigar and relaxed with the calm of a volcano waiting to explode. He blew greenish smoke in my face to show me who was boss, and I resisted the need to cough.

"I have the impression, Mr Shannon, that you have worked as a bodyguard before. Am I right?"

"I'm a private detective."

"Yes, but looking at the size of you, this must be work that you have taken on from time to time. How tall are you?"

"Big enough. I have done it in the past, but as I said, these days, I am strictly a private detective."

"Yes, I think we have established that, but what I need..." He hesitated as if he was searching for the right phrase. "What I require is somebody that will work for me as a bodyguard, but in a more, shall we say, creative way."

"You can say what you like, but I hire my services out as a detective."

"So, you would not consider being a bodyguard?"

"Creative bodyguard," I corrected. "Can you tell me what this is all about, sir?" I was losing patience and didn't like the oily expression on his face. He had the type of leer that was perfect for punching.

"At this moment, I am not sure exactly what type of protection I need, but it's the sort that would be more pro-active than defensive if you know what I mean."

"I don't."

"Do you carry a gun, Mr Shannon?"

"No. Aren't they illegal?"

"Not if you've got a licence. Do you have one?"

"No."

He tut, tutted, and shook his head. A mischievous smile erupted under his nose. "I'm sure we can get around that, Mr Shannon, if you are willing to work for me."

I needed the money but didn't like what I was hearing. I wished Shoddy had come with me. He was much better than I was at appraising clients and their intentions. Not all of them wanted your well-being. In fact, some of the clients I had worked for were as crooked and twisted as they come. I wasn't sure which category Hershey fitted into. I was about to find out.

"I was told about your services by an ex-client of yours."

"That narrows it down. Who?"

"The person that I spoke to didn't want his name to be mentioned, but he considers you to be the type of detective that is very flexible in the way that he works."

"There you go using intellectual words again. What exactly do you mean by flexible and pro-active?"

"I mean that I'm the type of person who thinks attack is the best form of defence. I am being attacked at this moment by somebody that wants to do me harm. Do me harm for something that I haven't done. I want this person to be taught a lesson. A lesson that will stop him and get him off my back."

"Does the name Rufus Dixon ring any bells, Mr Hershey?"

"You know him?" He filled his glass again and drained it in one huge gulp.

"I talked to him a few minutes ago, and he asked me to give you a message."

"I don't want to listen to any message from that man." He slurred

"I'll tell you anyway. He said that he needed to talk to you about his daughter. He also said that it was urgent."

"This man is preposterous. He seems to think that I have something to do with the disappearance of his daughter."

"And do you?"

"Of course, I don't."

"Do you know his daughter?"

"Yes, we have met, but I don't know anything about what happened to her or even if she has disappeared. If I were her, I would be hiding from him. Her father is totally mad. He has this fixation with me. I fear for my life, Mr Shannon, and that's where you come in."

"What do you want me to do?"

He smiled and relaxed. "That's the way, Mr Shannon. You've met the man. He is crazy, don't you think?"

I shrugged. "Depends on what has happened to his daughter."

He reached into his back pocket and brought out a wallet that was bulging with cash. "I can count out three thousand pounds as a down payment and give you another three thousand when the job is done."

"What job?"

"Rufus Dixon needs to disappear. Do you know what I am talking about?"

"I think I do, but can you be clearer?"

"He is never going to get it out of his head that I did something to his daughter. I didn't, but that's irrelevant to him. I am in fear for my life. I want you to take him out."

"Take him out where?"

"I think you are playing the Devil's Advocate here, Mr Shannon. Okay, I want you to arrange a little accident for him."

"Accident?"

"I want him dead. Can you do it?"

I got up and put my hat on. "No, I can't, and if I could, I wouldn't do it for a lousy six thousand pounds."

"I see. I will double it. Six thousand now and six thousand later. You have to make it look like an accident. Can you do that?"

Not for Twelve thousand."

"How about thirty thousand. You drive a very hard bargain, Mr Shannon. I am impressed. I will give you fifteen thousand pounds now and fifteen thousand when you have got rid of him."

I walked towards the door. "Can you let me out, Mr Hershey? I think I have heard enough."

"I thought your sort would do anything if the price were right."

I didn't answer him but stood holding my hat by the door while he opened it with his sweaty, podgy, doughboy fingers. As I made my way out, he snarled, "And don't tell anybody about our conversation. I will deny it and get you beaten up. Some people have lower standards than you and will do anything for cash in hand. Good day."

I have to admit; I was sweating when I got into the lift. Sweating and had worms writhing around in my gut. I never knew that people like Hershey existed, but I wondered how much influence the alcohol had on his manner. I also wondered what Shoddy was going to say.